Whispered Secrets

Rose Garden Apartments

Elizabeth Lennox

Copyright 2021
ISBN13: 9798724361958
All rights reserved

Table of Contents

Chapter 1

If a wounded soul needed a soft spot to land, this would be it.

Maggie Beauchamp sighed as she admired the Rose Garden Apartments. She'd done this, she thought to herself with pride. She'd restored these amazing historic buildings and revived the beauty that had been deteriorating through neglect and lack of funding.

She smiled as the sweet scent of her last yellow roses lifted their delicate blooms into the early morning sunshine. Fall was fast approaching, but her yellow roses were tough and wouldn't give up. The roses had been a gift from a previous resident and good friend, Lilly Hamilton...wait, no she was Lilly Gataki now. And she was about to give birth to her first child.

Sighing with happiness, Maggie pushed away from the telephone pole and walked back to her apartment. Yes, this was a good place for wounded souls, herself included. This place had healed her. It had made her a better person. At least, Maggie hoped that she was a better person now. She definitely hadn't been very nice a couple of years ago, but Maggie considered herself to be a work in progress. Just like these buildings.

Stretching her legs, she glanced over at the building across the street. The stucco buildings were chipped and filthy, covered in grime and graffiti. The previously beautiful landscaping was withered and choked with weeds, trash buried in the winding vines. The chipped sign for the building still stood, but the paint had faded from the sun, wind and rain, not to mention the miserable humidity that accompanied the intense heat every summer. Several of the apartment doors had been bashed in and replaced with plywood, which had then been marred with graffiti and gang symbols as well.

The small apartment complex was an eyesore for the neighborhood, but Maggie could see the potential in the structures. It could be brought back to life. Just like Rose Gardens, the bones were there. It just needed a soft touch, someone to care for the buildings.

Maybe that was going to happen. A "For Sale" sign had been nailed to the side of the building when Maggie had taken over here at Rose Gardens. Unfortunately, even that sign had faded, as if the property knew that no one would want such an old, beaten down place and had given up on even trying.

But now, there was a fresh "Sold" sign over the "For Sale" notice. Someone had bought the old beauty!

"Who bought you, my lady?" she whispered, still watching the worn out property as if it were an aging beauty queen. Unfortunately, there was no answer. Maggie felt a kinship with this neighborhood, and had since the first moment she's laid eyes on the place. The residents here had taken her in when she'd been so desperately sad and lost. They'd saved her. And she'd put just as much energy into saving them as well as saving these buildings.

Turning away from the beat up property, she surveyed the freshly painted, revitalized Rose Gardens Apartments. Unfortunately, something niggled at the back of her mind. Too many of the properties around the neighborhood had been bought up lately. It was a mystery, but hopefully, everything would turn out well in the end.

With a smile, she turned back, heading home. She waved to Mick as he stepped out from between the buildings, heading for his auto repair shop. Every day, six days a week, Mick trudged off to his shop two blocks away. He carried a cooler that contained his lunch and a thermos with his coffee, and worked on the cars that pulled into his shop, the neighborhood customers eager for Mick's expertise. The man could make a whole lot more money if he charged higher prices. But Mick considered his repair shop to be his way of helping out the neighborhood. And he really was a genius with anything mechanical. Most of the residents of this neighborhood couldn't afford a new car, so Mick kept the old ones running and kept his prices low, so that the residents could afford to get to work every day and put food on their tables for the kids.

A good man, Maggie thought, relieved that the renovations on his apartment were finally finished.

Speaking of men, she thought, pausing and glancing over at the building next door. Who was the guy walking along the balcony? He wore jeans and a hard hat, flannel shirt and work boots. But from this distance, she couldn't see his face. Still, Maggie got the sense that this man was...not wounded. She tilted her head, trying to gauge his temperament. No, he wasn't wounded, like so many of the residents around here.

Angry. Yes, that was the right word. The man was angry. His movements were jerky, almost impatient.

Was he a construction worker? Maggie knew that several of the construction companies in this area didn't treat their employees well. They cheated their workers out of hourly wages, stripped them of benefits, and fired them as soon as someone came along that would work for a lower wage.

Was this guy looking for a place to sleep? Maggie's heart lurched at the thought of someone in need. A few years ago, Maggie would have ignored someone that scruffy looking. She would have turned away and headed for the nail salon. Someone that desperate would have been beneath her notice.

Her life was a wee bit different these days. So instead of turning around and going about her business, she pivoted towards the abandoned building. It wasn't safe for that man to be in there, and too many people had been using those abandoned apartments for a place to sleep.

"Can I help you?" she called out, having lost sight of the guy after he'd stepped into one of the apartments.

The man stepped out of the apartment and Maggie gasped. This wasn't a vagrant looking for a place to crash. This man was...goodness, he was hot! Scruffy, definitely. But still...magnificently gorgeous! The dark hair was mussed, as if he'd run his hands through it repeatedly. There was about two days' worth of beard hiding what was most likely a square, hard jawline. High cheekbones and light, blue eyes that were...um...glaring at her?

Why would this man be angry with her? She'd done nothing wrong!

"Who are you?" the man demanded.

Maggie pulled back, startled by the rage in his tone. "I'm Maggie Beauchamp," she replied, folding her arms protectively over her stomach. "And you are?"

"Oliver," he snapped. Those dark eyebrows lowered over impressively blue eyes. "What are you doing here?"

He tucked his hard hat under his arm, then ran a hand over his face, sighing deeply, as if he hadn't slept in a long, long time. That sigh only reinforced the impression that the guy was homeless and that he was looking for a place to sleep. And maybe a place to hide?

At the fatigue around his eyes, Maggie's heart melted. "You're exhausted, aren't you?" She ignored the startled look in his eyes. "I can tell that you're tired, and by the looks of your jeans, you haven't had a place to crash in a while." She figured he was ex-military, like Jimmy, another resident of Rose Gardens. Jimmy was a former Navy SEAL and…well, demons lurked in his memories. Dangerous, horrible demons. And he was wounded deep down in his soul. Hurt in ways that he'd struggled for several years to heal. Living off of his military pension, Jimmy had struggled with alcohol addiction. Slowly, Jimmy was fighting his way out of the nightmares in his head. The man hadn't had a drink in over a year now. But every day was a struggle.

Maggie straightened her shoulders back and eyed the man carefully. He was definitely muscular. Probably just recently released from the military. And if he was looking around here for a place to sleep, it was just a small sidestep into the dangers of addiction.

No way! Not another one! Maggie wasn't letting another veteran fall into the depths of despair and addiction. She was going to help this man and give him a way out.

"You're tired, Oliver. And I'm sure that you're hungry." She took his arm and led him down the stairs. "This place is a mess and isn't fit to live in. But I have a place that you can stay tonight." She felt the resistance in his arm, but tightened her grip, towing him along.

Those startling blue eyes narrowed down at her. "Lady, I don't know what–"

"I know," she interrupted, patting his arm comfortingly. Wow, the guy had muscles! Big, solid muscles! "You're strong now. And you think you can do this alone. But you can't. I've seen it in others and I won't let you go down the same path!"

"What path?" he asked, still following her, but with a confused look to his handsome, all-American features.

"The path of self-destruction," she explained earnestly. "Jimmy can help you. And maybe you can help Jimmy. He's ex-military too, but he's working hard to pull himself together. You can too. If you haven't gone down that path, then he'll help you to stay away."

Oliver blinked down at the impassioned woman tugging at him, not sure what the hell was going on. There were more than a few things that he should probably address in her passionate speech, but he wasn't sure where to start. Besides, she was cute! Damn cute! And those tight leggings and sports jacket hugged her figure, showcasing a pair of long legs, a very fine ass, and a pair of perfectly shaped breasts that looked to be just the right size to fill his hands.

While his thoughts lingered on her delectable figure, he tried to stop their forward momentum. But the little woman was stronger than she looked. And she was determined to save him from…something, although Oliver still wasn't sure what. Also, who was this "Jimmy" person that would help him?

Curious now, they crossed the street and walked down a sidewalk lined with beautiful landscaping on both sides. Oliver was so confused but he wanted to understand, which was the only reason he allowed this adorable female to lead him to...somewhere. Tearing his eyes away from her soft lips, he realized that she was guiding him towards the Rose Garden Apartments, the only few buildings in this neighborhood that had any semblance of maintenance.

"Here," she said, pulling out a set of keys. "This apartment hasn't been renovated yet, so it's a bit of a mess. The previous tenant left a bed and some furniture. I can get you sheets and towels from the Center." She glanced at his jeans and Oliver's mind blanked again. It took all of his remaining mental resources after the last few days of exhaustive meetings to not reveal how strongly this woman's touch affected him.

For someone so small, she had a powerful presence. Her pulling and tugging...well, he wasn't sure why he was allowing it, other than because he was...fascinated and curious. Yep, that had to be it. The woman intrigued him.

Why the hell did she think that he needed a place to live though?

"I'll get you some clean clothes too."

Oliver glanced down at his jeans and...granted, they were a bit thread-bare in spots. And covered in smudges and dirt because he'd been inspecting that dump across the street. But these were his favorite jeans. Plus, he'd been exploring the abandoned apartments, which were filthy, making notes and mentally planning his next move.

"That's...very kind of you," he said, surprised by her passion, even if he was still confused. She obviously had no idea about his personal net worth.

And damn, that was refreshing!

The pretty woman snorted dismissively. Obviously, she didn't consider herself to be very kind.

Waving a hand towards the apartment's dim interior, she lifted her anxious gaze to his face. "Will this work?"

Oliver looked around, noting the boxes off to one side and a tattered sofa that had seen better days. There was an air of disrepair everywhere in this place. It was nothing like his penthouse downtown, which had been decorated by a celebrated designer just a year ago. His penthouse had every imaginable luxury and massive windows that let in the light, plus a large balcony where he could look out at the city.

And yet, somehow, he felt comfortable here in this deteriorating mess.

"Yeah. I–"

Those green eyes sparkled with relief, leaving him speechless for a moment.

"Good!" she interrupted before he could tell her that he didn't need a place to live.

"Do you need a job? If you do, then I can probably help you there too." She stepped into the kitchen. "The owner of this apartment complex is a wonderful man. He's authorized the renovation of every apartment. So if you're looking for work, I'm sure he'd hire you to help out with the renovations."

A job? He almost laughed. Oliver's development company employed over thirty thousand people. At any point in time, he had approximately one hundred projects under construction around the globe. Vendors fought tooth and nail to work for him, and yet, this little woman was offering him a job as a part time construction worker?

He felt as if he'd stepped into an alternative universe!

"I...uh...I have a job," he told her, not exactly sure what to say. She was pretty, sexy, *and* kind?

Yep, definitely an alternative universe. That was the only explanation that made sense. He'd stepped into a time warp somehow and this gorgeous woman was a test to see if he could make heads or tails out of this new world.

"Well, of course you do," she agreed easily, and he could tell by the look in her eyes that she didn't believe him. Were his clothes really that bad? He ran a hand over his face, trying to hide his amusement. But his hand ran over the scruff that he hadn't bothered to shave this morning. Granted, he hadn't showered this morning either, knowing that he would be exploring filthy spaces. And his clothes obviously showed that those old apartments had been dirtier than anticipated. But she thought he was homeless and jobless?

No wait...she thought he was an ex-military guy down on his luck and heading towards self-destruction. Drugs and alcohol? Nope! Okay, yeah, he enjoyed a good glass of wine or a great scotch on occasion. But drugs? Never! Her words were slowly starting to filter into his lust-boggled mind. He wanted to laugh. Hell, he wanted to pull her into his arms and kiss her!

But he pulled back, evaluating the situation with a large dose of cynicism. No one was *this* nice. This was a test. A trick, perhaps. Looking around, he wondered if he was being punked. Were there hidden cameras somewhere?

"Um...I'm not sure that...?"

Apparently, she wasn't finished. The beauty lifted her hand, her forefinger pointed towards the cracked ceiling. "Oh, and tonight, its hot dogs and s'mores out by the fire pit."

His eyes widened with surprise. S'mores? He hadn't had s'mores since he'd been a Boy Scout, way back in elementary school.

Her eyes widened. "I mean, the s'mores and hot dogs are...they're complex issues." She closed her eyes and did a slight head shake. "Not complex as in complicated," she went on to explain, obviously flustered. "I meant, the hot dogs and s'mores are for the apartment complex." She blinked, mentally going over her words, then shook her head again. "For the residents, not the building. Buildings don't eat s'mores," she felt the need to explain. "Or hot dogs." Once again, the lovely, adorable woman closed her eyes for a moment and sighed heavily.

Oliver swallowed a laugh. Something told him that any show of amusement might be taken as an insult by this prickly beauty.

She shuffled her feet and explained, not looking him in the eye now. "I'm not asking you out," she said, as a soft, pink stain moved up her neck to her cheeks. "Not that you aren't handsome! You are, and..." her gaze moved slowly over his body, taking it all in, and Oliver gritted his teeth to keep himself from showing how much he wanted her to ask him out. Not just on a date. But to her bed! "You're a very handsome man and obviously take excellent care of yourself. You've probably done a lot of wonderful things for our country, which is why you've kept your body in such..." she stopped, seeming to trip over her words. Was she actually going to say it?

Damn, she sighed and Oliver could tell that she was mentally backing away. Damn, she was cute! And hot! He could see her nipples as they pressed against the thin material of her shirt.

Finally, she opened her eyes and bowed her head. "I'm really making a muck of this, aren't I? And embarrassing us both in the process. I'm so sorry," she told him, taking a step back. "Seriously, I'm not trying to force you into taking this apartment. I just want to help. If you want the place, then the rent is pretty affordable." She named a price that made Oliver cough in surprise. How the hell could the owner maintain a profit margin charging so little? And renovating the apartments? At that price? Maybe the rent increased after the apartments were updated. He'd been hearing rumors about Rose Gardens Apartments, which is why he'd started looking around this neighborhood. As a developer, Oliver could tell this neighborhood was perfect for a regeneration project. Which is why he'd quietly started buying up as many of the surrounding properties as he could.

At his stunned look, she started to reach out to him, then pulled her hands back. "Is that too much? This is a special apartment building. So, if you can't afford it, say so. We can work something out."

"That's fine," he replied, shocking himself. What was "fine"? He wasn't moving in here! He had a ten thousand square foot penthouse about ten miles away! His place had extraordinary views and everything exactly the way he wanted it.

"Good!" she sighed, obviously relieved. "I'll have Eddie stop by and tell you about the renovations. He's not in charge, but since its Sunday, the workers are off. But Eddie works with the teams, so he can fill you in on the details."

Oliver nodded, confused and fascinated. Crossing his arms over his chest, he stared down at the woman, aware that he was making her nervous but not sure how to ease her worries. She was such a tiny thing, but those big green eyes were huge with emotions that she was obviously trying to hide.

"Well, if you have time tonight, we'd love to see you at the fire pit. All of us." Her hand fluttered out, encompassing the other apartments. "The residents, that is." She took a step backwards, moving carefully towards the doorway. "But if you can't make it, well, I'll understand. And..." she waved a hand at the boxes. "I'm sorry that this apartment isn't renovated. But we'll get it on the schedule as soon as we can."

Oliver continued to watch her, wondering who she was. Then he remembered her name. Maggie, he thought, repeating the name in his mind. Maggie Beauchamp. He thought about making a call to his security chief and having him work up a dossier on her. But the idea left a bad taste in his mouth. No, he wouldn't use his vast resources on this mysterious woman.

He wanted to discover her secrets himself. Not that she could have all that many, he thought with a chuckle as she pulled the door closed, stumbling on the threshold as she hurried away. Unlike his past relationships, Oliver wanted his knowledge of Maggie Beauchamp to come to him the old fashioned way. Through conversation and time.

He watched as the beauty walked away, more fascinated than he'd ever been by a woman.

Time? What the hell? Oliver didn't have "spare time". It was a Sunday morning and he had about ten thousand things to get done by the end of the day. He'd come out here to investigate the building he'd just purchased, to inspect the vacant apartments as well as the neighborhood, and develop a plan of attack. He owned pretty much all of the buildings within an eight block radius now. Oliver planned to tear them all down and build sky rise buildings that would include multi-use areas like condominiums, retail spaces, and office areas.

At least, that was the current plan. His idea was to create a whole new go-to area here on the edge of Crystal City. It was a prime spot for building and was ripe for a whole new look. The new Amazon headquarters had just moved in about four miles away. This was a perfect spot for condos and office spaces, new restaurants and bars, nightclubs and...hell, it was exceptionally situated for his plans.

So, what the hell was he doing standing here in this decrepit apartment that needed a whole new lighting system as well as new flooring, cabinets, and...the appliances looked to be at least forty years old! He should get out of here and head back to his car, which was parked over on the other side of the building next door. His Maserati stuck out like a sore thumb in this area and would be a prime temptation for car thieves.

And yet, instead of leaving and getting back to work, Oliver walked slowly through the apartment, mentally noting all of the areas that needed to be fixed and updated. The pale pink tiles in the bathroom were clean-ish, but had probably been installed back in the sixties. They'd obviously been re-grouted at some point, because the grout was relatively clean. But there were gaps in the grout, which would cause problems if water seeped behind the tiles. The floor tiles were an odd shade of avocado green. Hmm...pink and green bathroom. Not the best combination. The bathroom vanity was outdated as well, but had been made from solid wood, so only parts of it were dry rotted. He flipped the switch for the bathroom fan, but nothing happened. Looking up, he noticed the well rusted fan, which should have been thrown away decades ago.

He wandered into the bedroom, surprised to find a large mattress that didn't seem too dirty. He didn't relish the idea of sleeping on a stranger's bed though. The closet doors were off the hinges and...okay actually, the hinges were gone. The doors were in good shape, but again, they were bi-fold doors that had gone out of style decades ago. A pair of "barn doors" would look good in here. And would be easier to use. The windows were smallish, but with trim and the right kind of windows installed, they could look funky instead of dated.

He returned to the kitchen. The linoleum flooring was scraped and faded, even ripped in several places. Someone had tried to glue the tears back down, but dirt had accumulated in the gash over the years and the edges were dark with grime. The cabinets were the worst though. Several of the doors were hanging from broken hinges, there was rot in several corners, the stove didn't look as if it would actually work and...the refrigerator should be moved into the bathroom, where it matched the floor. The avocado green fridge was...well, some might call it quaint. He thought it looked pathetic. A remnant of a bygone era that, thankfully, hadn't lasted long.

"What the hell are you doing here?" he muttered to himself, standing in the middle of the kitchen/den area that was separated only by an L shaped countertop. With his hands fisted on his hips, he shook his head in disgust. "You have work to do."

  With that, he headed towards the doorway, determined to set Ms. Maggie Beauchamp straight. Maybe he'd ask her out for dinner. He could take her to that Italian restaurant that had just opened up down in DuPont Circle. She'd like it. Lots of ambiance and the food was excellent.

  So, why did he hesitate at the door? Why did he turn around and, swearing under his breath, grab the key before leaving? What the hell was he thinking?!

Chapter 2

Six hours later, Maggie watched with jittery anticipation as the residents gathered around the fire pit. Eddie had been the first to arrive and had helped her set up the small table and lay out the food.

She'd gotten the cushions out of the storage room, pretty flowered and plaid cushions that Louise and Nora had sewed over the past several months.

"This looks real nice, Maggie," Eddie had announced once everything was ready.

"Thanks," she sighed, trying to relax. He was just a guy, she reminded herself. Just another resident. Someone who needed a little help. Maggie loved helping people. So, this guy was a good fit for her. He needed help and she needed to help. A match made in heaven.

So, why was she so nervous?

"He'll be here," Eddie muttered, handing her a cold soda before walking away.

"Who will be here?" she asked, trying to feign a casualness that she didn't feel.

"Is he here?" Louise asked, walking over to the food table and helping herself to an orange soda and a Dr. Pepper for Nora.

"Who?" Maggie asked.

Nora chuckled as she expertly popped the top off of her soda bottle on the edge of the new brick fire pit that Eddie and Jimmy had built. "That gorgeous hunk of man that you brought in earlier today," Nora replied with mock frown at Maggie for daring to feign ignorance.

Maggie cleared her throat. "That's Oliver..." she paused, shaking her head. "Actually, I don't know his last name yet. But he seems nice. Fresh out of the military and looking a little lost. More than slightly rough around the edges." She took a sip of her soda. "He just needs a

11

bit of help to get back on track."

Nora and Louise nodded. "Then he came to the right place. We'll help him out!" both ladies announced.

Maggie smiled weakly, looking back towards the still-closed door nervously. Would he show up? Or had he left already?

She turned her attention back to Louise. "Thanks. Could you mention Oliver's predicament to Jimmy too? I think they might have a lot in common. They both have that 'warrior' vibe about them."

Mick nodded in agreement. "Good idea, honey," he said as he picked up one of the metal fire-pokers, sliding a hot dog onto the end before moving towards the fire so that he could roast his dinner.

Oliver stood back in the shadows, admiring the scene. The residents were chatting happily in small groups, many of them roasting hot dogs and marshmallows over the dancing fire while sipping soda or beer. Some had brought lawn chairs while others spread themselves across the pillow-strewn benches. There were strings of lights overhead, adding more light as well as a festive air to the scene.

This was nice, he thought. This was a community. It seemed as if everyone knew each other and, even more importantly, cared about one another. He couldn't remember the last time he'd spoken to...or even passed...anyone in his current building. Having a private elevator and private parking area gave him a sense of isolation from the other residents where he lived. Up until this moment, he'd always appreciated that his wealth could allow him to separate himself from the rest of the world. He worked long hours so when he came home, he didn't want to be bothered with polite conversations at the mail box or in the elevator.

But these people were gathered around, talking and laughing among themselves, teasing each other but doing it in a gentle, friendly way. As Oliver lingered in the shadows, observing and listening, he didn't hear a single malicious comment.

And he had to admit that the hot dogs smelled pretty damn good. He'd never been the type to enjoy carnival foods before, but smelling the dogs roasting on the wood fire brought back memories.

He approached the food-laden table, adding a case of cold beer that he'd picked up, correctly assuming that everyone would contribute something to the evening's festivities.

"Are you him?" some guy asked eagerly. The man had dark skin and dark hair with white streaks at the temples.

"Him?" Oliver repeated, not sure if he was the "him" in question or not.

"Oliver!" Maggie exclaimed, rushing over to him. He noticed that she didn't have a hot dog in her hands. Just a glass of lemonade. Cute, he thought. When was the last time he'd enjoyed lemonade? Maybe he'd had some with a dash of vodka in it but only because one of his previous lovers had forced him to try her rather idiotic martinis. But pure, unadulterated lemonade?

"Am I late?" he asked, still wondering what he was doing here. He'd changed into an old, but clean college tee shirt and a clean pair of jeans. Normally, he would be dressed in khaki slacks and a button down shirt. But Oliver hadn't wanted to lose Maggie's perception that he was a lost soul, looking for redemption and salvation.

"Nope! We're just early," she replied, grabbing a reusable plastic cup and pouring him some lemonade.

"I brought beer," he told her.

Those emerald eyes faltered and she pulled back, startled. "Oh. Right! I'm sure that you'd prefer beer instead of...well, I'm just being silly I guess," she finally stammered. Still, she nervously eyed the case of beer.

Immediately, Oliver realized where her thoughts had gone. She was worried about Oliver diving into alcohol to soothe his inner wounds. In that moment, he wanted to please her. So instead of grabbing one of the cold beers, he nodded to the cup she was still holding. "But the lemonade sounds like a much better choice," he smiled.

Maggie's smile was almost brighter than the fire now. She gazed up into his eyes and, for some silly reason, Oliver felt like a hero.

He wasn't a hero though, he thought. As soon as Maggie discovered that he was the bastard buying up all the abandoned buildings and land in the neighborhood, and would slowly tear them all down to make room for bigger and better buildings, she'd never look at him again.

So right now, he was going to revel in her smile and enjoy himself. The time will come when he'd have to be honest with her. But right now, her smile eased the tension in his shoulders. Tension that he hadn't been aware of until it disappeared.

"Jimmy!" she called out.

An older man, slightly stooped, and wearing a clean pair of baggy khaki slacks and a tee shirt that had seen better days, came over to them. But as Oliver looked into the man's eyes, there was something there. A struggle. His wounds clearly ran deep. Oliver remembered Maggie's comment about Jimmy being a former Navy SEAL. But behind the pain lurking in the man's steady gaze was something else. Something stronger. His gaze was straight, even though his shoulders were a bit crooked, as if protecting himself from the world. Strength. Integrity. The man looked right back at Oliver as if daring him to judge.

Oliver extended his hand, his respect increasing when Jimmy shook his hand with a solid shake.

"You're the new guy?" Jimmy asked.

"I guess I am," Oliver replied.

Jimmy looked Oliver over, as if the older man could see into his soul. For a long moment, Oliver wondered if Jimmy was going to see the truth and reveal it to the others. Of course, Oliver hadn't *actually* lied. But he hadn't corrected Maggie's belief that Oliver was destitute and in desperate need of saving. Still, Oliver didn't want the truth of his wealth revealed. Not yet. He needed...time.

Instead, Jimmy glanced over at Maggie, who was working the crowd like a professional, offering potato salad and coleslaw to those who already had hot dogs. When Jimmy glanced up at Oliver again, there was understanding in the man's eyes. Understanding and intelligence.

Oliver didn't consider himself to be easy to read. In fact, several business articles had commented on how no one knew what was going on in Oliver's business world until Oliver decided to reveal it. So, what was it about Jimmy that allowed him to see what so many others missed?

Oliver glanced at Maggie, then back to Jimmy. The other man nodded easily, then walked away, sitting closer to the fire.

Confused by Jimmy's odd acceptance and...approval? Yes, it was definitely approval. Whatever, Oliver turned, watching Maggie who appeared to be avoiding him. Interesting, he thought as he caught her sideways glance before she quickly looked away. Taking a sip of the lemonade, he was surprised at how delicious it was.

"She's a good person," a female voice interrupted Oliver's thoughts.

He turned and found a pretty blond with pale skin that seemed to glow in the light coming from the fire standing beside him.

"Are you referring to Maggie?" he asked.

The woman scoffed. "As if you've noticed anyone else here tonight?"

Oliver conceded her point with a faint smile. "I'm Oliver," he said, extending his hand.

"Molly," the blond woman announced, taking his hand with a firm handshake. "Maggie mentioned that you might need a little help." She pulled her eyes away from the woman in question and looked up at Oliver. "You really don't look like someone who needs help."

Stunned, Oliver couldn't halt the bark of laughter, thinking the woman was quite perceptive. "I've been known to need a helping hand occasionally."

Molly's head tilted slightly, eyeing Oliver carefully. "You're not ex-military either, are you?"

Damn, she was good. "No. I fully support our men and women in uniform, but I've never served in the military myself."

"Didn't think so." They both turned to watch Maggie, who had picked up a plate of cookies and was offering them around. "Interesting," Molly commented, then turned to look quizzically up at Oliver. "Are you going to hurt her?"

"Maggie?" he asked, shocked that anyone would be that direct. Especially with him. People usually treated him with kid gloves, terrified of his wrath. He'd been known to destroy his competition without a second thought.

"Is there anyone *else* here you can't keep your eyes off of?" the woman teased.

Oliver again conceded her point. "I have never planned to hurt anyone."

Molly didn't think that was good enough and she frowned, her gaze turning hard. "She's gone through a great deal," she explained. "I don't know the story, or even most of the details, but I do know that she's a good person. Maggie doesn't think so, but everyone else loves her. And we watch out for her, just as she watches out for us." Molly stepped closer, pinning him with her sharp gaze. "If you do *anything* to hurt her, you'll have us to deal with. You don't want that."

And then she was gone. Oliver watched as Molly settled next to Mick and handed him something that Oliver couldn't identify from across the fire, but Mick seemed delighted.

Oliver contemplated the pretty woman who had just threatened him. She appeared to be a bit of fluff. But Oliver now saw the strength inside of her. He realized that Molly wasn't offering idle threats. Every one of these residents looked out for each other. If something happened to one of them, it happened to all of them.

Turning, his eyes once again clashed with the one woman he couldn't seem to stop thinking about. All day, he'd told himself that he should stay away. That Maggie was untarnished. She was good, kind, and generous. She'd taken in a stranger that she'd thought needed help. In reality, Oliver was the kind of man that could hurt her deeply.

But he wouldn't, he vowed. Not Maggie. No, she was too pure. Too sweet and kind.

Yes, he should walk away and leave her in peace. But for some reason, he couldn't seem to force his feet to go. He couldn't just walk away from Maggie. There was just something about her, something innately good and kind that...he needed. It was more than just her luscious curves and those brilliant eyes. He craved *her*.

Maggie watched, wanting to screech her fury and claw at Molly's eyes. But Molly was her friend! Molly was one of the best!

But Molly had flirted with Oliver, a man Maggie had already mentally claimed for herself.

Not that he'd allowed that claiming. In reality, Maggie had no real claim on the man. He was simply another resident. Another person she could take care of. And yes, Oliver needed a bit of caring too. He was big and tough and there was a strength in him that she recognized. But there was something else inside of him that was wounded. Just like the others, Oliver needed her. Now that Molly was sitting next to Mick and that green-eyed monster had moved away, Maggie could see that need in Oliver's eyes.

Walking over to him, she offered the platter of cookies. "Louise makes the best butterscotch cookies around," she explained. "Would you like to try one?"

Oliver stared into Maggie's eyes as he took one of the cookies. "The best?" he asked, teasing her in the hopes of seeing another blush. Unfortunately, Maggie had her back to the fire, so he couldn't really see her expression. Pity, he thought.

"Yes. She and Nora used to own a bakery down the street. They ran it for about forty years until they retired."

"And now they make cookies for occasions like this?"

"Oh, no!" Maggie grinned. "They bake for just about any reason." Maggie leaned forward conspiratorially. "Don't stub your toe, or you'll get a batch of something within a few hours." She leaned back. "I swear, I've gained weight since taking on this job because of Nora and Louise's baking."

He took a bite and...holy cow! He blinked down at the cookie, stunned by the burst of flavors. "These are incredible!" he said, startled by how good they really were. He'd been expecting an old fashioned cookie with too much flour or maybe too sweet. But the cookie was rich and warm and bursting with butterscotch flavor, as well as a warm, gooey center. "Damn, these are amazing!"

Maggie laughed. "Told ya," she replied, swinging her shoulders back and forth slightly. "So, are you going to take the job?"

Oliver swallowed and considered taking another cookie. Or maybe a dozen more! They were that good!

"I already have a job, but–"

"You can work part time. Eddie is a wonderful manager."

"I'll think about it," he promised because he doubted that Maggie would accept no for an answer. She wanted to make sure he was financially set. So he could pay the rent? No, he suspected that her hopes ran deeper than simple financial security.

"Why is the rent so low here?" he asked, curious despite himself.

Maggie's eyes glowed with pride as she glanced around at the fire-lit courtyard. "Because this is a special place. I made a deal with the owner, Drako Gataki. He agreed to keep the rent low and he even covered the cost of the renovations. In exchange, we all help out around the neighborhood." She beamed, "It's a massive tax write off for him. In the end, it's a win-win situation for everyone. The residents get a decent place to live at a reasonable price. They don't have to move further outside the city and they don't have to deal with long commutes. In return, we all figure out ways to keep the operating costs low, so that Drako can at least turn a small profit."

"That's very generous of him," Oliver commented, thinking that perhaps he'd have a chat with the guy. Oliver had seen Drako at the gala at the Kennedy Center last weekend, along with his very pregnant, incredibly beautiful wife. They'd both looked nauseatingly happy and Oliver remembered glancing at Desiree and...no, his relationship with Desiree was in the past. It was over and he'd moved on.

Coming back to the present, he looked down at Maggie. "An interesting business model," Oliver replied. "I've read about Drako Gataki. He's not a man who lets a good business deal get away."

"Oh, he's a very generous man. Very sweet too! I'm good friends with Lilly. In fact, Molly and I had lunch with her about two days ago."

Ah! A personal friend of Drako's wife. That made sense now.

"So he does all of this out of the goodness of his heart?"

Maggie laughed as if the idea was ridiculous. "No way! He wants a profit. We just figure out how to make that happen. I select the residents here, both for their needs as well as how their talents might benefit the community." She looked at him triumphantly. "You're a good addition."

His eyebrows lifted at that announcement. "How am I supposed to help?"

Maggie poked his bicep playfully. "Eh, you're the pretty boy who's going to keep the bad guys at bay."

That was startling news to him. She thought he could fight off bad guys? For some reason, his chest puffed up with that news. "I'll do my best. But who are the bad guys? Do you have trouble with gangs around here?"

He didn't like the idea of gangs causing problems with his development projects. So if there were a serious gang issue, he'd have to work with the local police to develop a plan.

"Oh, you'd be surprised at the problems that we have around here.

But no, the gangs aren't the big issue," she told him. "And besides, sometimes it's the people you don't suspect who become the biggest worry."

"Who are your bad guys?" he asked, his tone softening because he liked being her hero. He'd never been anyone's hero before and it was a heady sensation.

The light in her eyes dimmed and Oliver wanted to kick himself for asking such a sad question.

"Sometimes, the bad guys are right next door," she replied, and there was a sadness, a pain, to her words, that alerted him that she was telling a truth that was too deep for her to acknowledge. She forced her lips to smile. "And sometimes, it's the rich guys that are a problem." She leaned closer. "Rich guys can be absolute assholes!"

He was so startled by her words that he froze for a moment. Then he threw back his head, laughing. Yeah, the wealthy weren't particularly merciful when it came to steam rolling over certain aspects of one's life. Himself in particular, he knew.

"Well, I'll see what I can do to protect you from the gangs as well as wealthy assholes," he vowed. Oliver had used a teasing tone, but deep down inside, he was absolutely serious. Even if it meant protecting her from himself.

Her melodic laugh touched him deeply and, even in the dim light, he could see the sparkle in her eyes. "That's a valiant offer, sir," she said, then dipped into a small curtsy as if she were a fair maiden. He laughed as well, delighted with her casual teasing and light banter.

Oliver never realized how tired he was of the social scene in which he traveled. Speaking to people at the numerous events he attended was like maneuvering through a chess game. He was one of the best players, but standing here in the firelight, he realized how sick he was of the games and the pathetic innuendos he usually had to deal with. This was nice, he thought. Just mild flirting…okay serious flirting on his part…and casual conversation about nothing more important than the best way to bake a cookie or slay monsters. There were no undercurrents of animosity running through the low hum of conversation with these people. The only bursts were occasional laughter.

As the evening wore on, people drifted away, waving as they each made their way back to their homes.

Oliver stayed back, sitting on one of the benches since he hadn't thought to bring a lawn chair. He'd remember next time. But right now, he was more interested in watching Maggie as she flitted around, picking up the remnants of their small party.

"What can I do to help?" he asked, standing up and moving towards her.

He watched, fascinated as she clutched the empty platter against her chest. "Oh. Um...nothing. I have everything under control."

He looked around. Everyone had cleaned up the majority of the mess. There was just the folding table to put away and the bags of garbage that needed to be taken to the dumpster.

"I'll get the table and break it down. Where does it go?"

Maggie bit her lip, and shook her head. "Oh, you don't have to do that. It's my job. I'll take care of it."

He lifted an eyebrow. "Where does it go, Maggie?" he repeated in a firmer tone now.

She laughed, the sound tinkling through the darkness. "Oh, you think you're going to do your he-man role now?"

He leaned forward. "If doing a he-man thing involves putting away the plastic folding table, then yeah. I'm gonna do it."

Her smile relaxed and he wanted to move closer. But there was something in her eyes and in the way she held the platter against her, like a shield, he thought, that warned him to back off. He thought about her comment about wounded souls. Was she one of those souls?

He didn't like the idea of anyone hurting Maggie. She was so sweet and kind and, if he ever discovered whoever had hurt her, Oliver vowed that he'd destroy the person.

"What just happened, Oliver?" Maggie asked, stepping forward and abandoning the platter on the table beside her.

"What do you mean?" he asked, wanting to reach out and pull her closer, put his hands on her hips and feel her softness against his chest.

"You went somewhere," she whispered, worry in her gaze. "Something bad just went through your mind, right? Are you okay?"

She lifted her hand, carefully touching his cheek and he could feel her fingers like a flame, bursting upon his brain. Immediately, he was on fire, wanting this tiny woman and all of her passionate concern. But he didn't want her worried about him. No, Oliver knew he wanted her passion. Not her worries.

Decision made, he nodded, carefully keeping his hands at his sides. "I'm fine. I was just thinking about the person who had hurt you."

Blinking, she stepped back. "I'm not hurt," she told him, but her shoulders curled inward.

"You're a very strong woman, Maggie. But someone hurt you. Who was it?"

She shook her head and turned away. "I'm fine, Oliver. Please, you don't need to worry about me." She bent down and lifted the cardboard box. "They drank all of your beer!"

He laughed and took the box, crushing it so it would fit into the recycling bin. "That's why I brought it. I'm glad everyone enjoyed it."

"But…" she hesitated, turning around to sift through the other items, stuffing serving spoons and platters into what appeared to be a storage bin for just that purpose. "You didn't have a drink, did you?"

Oliver considered her question. Yeah, he should be offended that Maggie thought he was an alcoholic. But it felt actually pretty damn nice to have someone concerned about him. It felt good. Really good. Normally, he was the person with the weight of everyone's lives on his shoulders. Having someone worry about him for a change was… incredible!

He carefully maintained his distance as he said, "I promise that, if I feel as if I'm losing control and will drink to excess, I'll find you first, okay?"

Her shoulders relaxed and she sighed with relief. "Sounds like a deal."

He helped her finish cleaning up. When she reached for the folding table, he shook his head. "I know that you're strong enough to do this by yourself, Maggie. But while I'm here, I'm going to insist on doing it for you."

She stepped back, rolling her eyes playfully. But there was a smile to her soft, full lips as well. "Thank you," she replied.

"Tell me where to put it."

She pointed towards the last apartment in the building. "I've taken over one of the un-renovated apartments as a temporary storage area. You can put it in there."

He nodded, then carried it easily to the door. Once it was put away, he pulled the door closed, made sure the lock clicked, then turned around to find Maggie lifting the storage bin. Hurrying over, he grabbed it out of her hands and shook his head. "You'll learn eventually," he growled.

Maggie smiled, then led the way to her apartment. "This way."

He followed, and waited while she unlocked the door. He stood there for a long moment, just watching her. She was nervous and he thought that was a good thing. Hell, it was the only indication that she was just as affected by this lust as he was. And boy did he like that!

"I'll take it from here," she told him, reaching for the box.

"Just tell me where to put it, Maggie," he repeated, lifting it out of her reach.

She sighed, shook her head, then stepped back. "Just put it in the first bedroom," she told him, pointing.

Oliver moved quickly through the apartment, barely looking around. He got the impression that Maggie didn't want him in here for some reason. So he was going to respect that wish. But his curiosity burned.

He set the box down in the room and barely glanced at the stacks of other boxes surrounding a desk. This was obviously her office. He backed out and headed for the front door.

"All set," he told her, stepping outside.

"Thank you, Oliver," she told him, toying with her keys nervously.

"I'll let you get some sleep," he said. A moment later, he walked away and forced himself to walk into his apartment, without looking back at her. It was one of the hardest, longest walks of his entire life!

Chapter 3

"When are you going to forgive me, Oliver?"

Oliver sighed and fought the urge to roll his eyes. It had been two days since he'd seen or spoken to Maggie, so this interruption by his former lover only made his temper simmer even hotter.

Still, Desiree was good at her job, even if he didn't want to continue an affair. In retrospect, he hadn't wanted the affair to begin with. Desiree had sort of...well, he wasn't sure how the relationship had started. Giving Desiree Milken any sort of encouragement was tantamount to flaming her own bizarre belief that their relationship was just on pause.

"Do you have the latest progress reports for me?" he asked, not bothering to look up from the contract he was reviewing.

She sighed dramatically and came around to his side of the desk, leaning gracefully back in a pose that Oliver knew showed off her figure to the best advantage.

"Oliver, how many times do I have to say I'm sorry?"

He shook his head and scribbled notes in the margins of the document. "You've apologized several times already. I've accepted your apology. Now, it's time to move on."

She huffed a bit and he knew the sound was his cue to look up at her. Instead, he kept his attention on the document and wondered how long until she would take the hint and get out.

"Oliver, seriously! This has gone on long enough! I've apologized. You say that you've accepted my apology. So let's just...get back to where we were before!"

Irritated, Oliver tossed the contract down onto his desk, trying to hide his disgust. "Desiree, you were having sex with my landscaping guy," he replied, not even angry about it anymore. And suddenly, he realized that he'd never really been angry about her infidelity. In fact, he'd almost anticipated it. Bed hopping was pretty much an accepted practice in their world. He didn't like it and, until this past weekend, he hadn't realized that he'd almost expected it of his future wife.

"It was just the one time!" she asserted, even though he suspected that was a lie. He wasn't sure how long the affair had been going on, but it had been more than just the one time.

"In my bed," he continued, barely glancing at her.

She shrugged. "Yeah, well, you weren't using it," she came right back.

Oliver's only reply was a sarcastic lifting of his dark eyebrow.

Desiree huffed again, pushing away from the desk and stomped dramatically around the office. Again, he knew that her movements were perfectly choreographed to best show off her figure. Oliver agreed, her figure was truly extraordinary. Desiree spent hours in the gym honing her body. She also spent a great deal of money at the spa getting her nails manicured and pedicured, facials and massages. He knew because, up until several weeks ago, he'd paid for all of it.

After he'd found her in his bed with another man, he'd cut up the credit cards he'd given her, taken back the engagement ring, and ordered her out of his house. Oliver gave the woman credit, she knew how to play this so it sounded like he was the unreasonable one. But he wasn't buying it.

She'd even left a bunch of stuff around his house. Small things, but items he knew that she'd want back, giving her the opportunity to enter his house and continue pleading her case. But Oliver had lived with the woman. He recognized her games and had circumvented her return by going through every room and gathering up those small items, then had his assistant mail them back. He hadn't even brought them here to the office to return to her. That would have required that he enter her office and, just having her work here was annoying enough.

Granted, she was extremely good at her job. As a publicist and marketing expert, Desiree knew how to make the most out of any phrase or picture. So as long as she did her job, he would respect her in the office. Outside of the office though, he didn't want to have anything to do with her.

"Oliver, seriously, you can't be *that* upset about this. It isn't as if we were having sex all that often anyway."

He rubbed the bridge of his nose. "So, you took it upon yourself to find an additional lover?" he offered. "Is that *really* where you're going with this?"

She stopped and frowned at him. "Well, it wasn't like that. I mean, it's not as if I went out and looked for someone to have sex with since you were too busy to come home."

He leaned back in his chair, eyeing her curiously. "How did we even get to that point?"

She blinked and stopped her fidgeting for a moment. "What do you mean?"

"How did it come to pass that you moved in and we were engaged?"

Desiree laughed, her mahogany hair sparkling in the sunshine streaming into his office. She truly was an extraordinarily beautiful woman. Fortunately, he wasn't even slightly attracted to her. Not anymore. Had he ever been?

"You asked me out. I agreed," she explained with a wave of her hand and her eyes lifted to look off to the right slightly, as if the memory was a dreamy one. "The rest is history."

His eyes narrowed on her. "If my memory is correct, *you* asked *me* out."

Desiree moved over to his bookcase and picked up a heavy object that his decorator had set in that spot. "Details."

He waited, needing to hear the rest of this. But when she simply hefted the object in her hands, maybe considering throwing it at his head, Oliver realized that Desiree wasn't going to continue. She had a specific version of their history in her mind, real or not, and she wasn't deviating from that script.

"Another point, I don't remember proposing."

She laughed and swung her long hair over her shoulder as she turned to face him again. "Oh, we'd agreed to get married. You bought me a ring and everything."

His lips twisted slightly. "That's not how I remember it. Seems to me, we were walking along the river one evening, passed by a jewelry store, and you dragged me inside. You pointed to a ring, said 'why not?' and suddenly, we were engaged. So, it seems as if you proposed to me and..." he thought back, "I'm not sure I actually agreed."

She chuckled. "You had to be led along the correct path," she agreed easily. "Which is why I'm not giving up on us, Oliver. We're good together."

"In what way?" he asked, truly mystified.

She pulled back. "What do you mean? In every way?"

He disagreed. "Desiree, are you *honestly* attracted to me?"

"Of course!" she scoffed. "Like I said, we make sense. Our families have been friends forever. We know the same people. We have the same goals." She sighed and braced her hands wide against his desk, leaning forward to give him a clear view of her breasts encased in a silver bra. "We want the same things."

Oliver looked at the view, but it left him cold. Incredible, since the thought of getting up early enough to go watch Maggie run tomorrow morning so that he could see her in another one of those tight, body hugging running outfits made his mind blank for a long moment.

Unfortunately, Desiree thought that his pause meant she'd won.

"We really don't," he told her flatly, being callous, unsure how else to get through to her that their relationship was over.

Her glossy lips curled into a triumphant smile. "Oh, I think we do, Oliver."

He sighed, irritated now. "Get out of my office. And don't ever come in here without an appointment again." With that dismissal, he stood up and walked out to his next meeting. But he paused at the door to speak with his assistant, Jamie. "Make sure that Desiree has an appointment with me the next time she wants to see me. But check with me before scheduling anything since the issues she usually discusses with me should most likely go through the marketing director."

"Of course, Oliver," Jamie replied. He saw the malicious gleam in Jamie's eyes as he walked away and wondered if Desiree had been more of a problem than he realized. Had she become a nuisance to the rest of the staff?

He'd have to keep an eye on her. Maybe have a conversation with her about treating the staff more politely. But right now, he didn't have proof that she was a nuisance. And right now, he had a meeting about tearing down a neighborhood that he was no longer convinced should be torn down.

Desiree watched the man she...well, he was hot, she acknowledged. But he was a *man.* Boring, pointless, and irritating. She'd hated how she'd had to trick Oliver into asking her out for dinner that first night. And yeah, he was right, the ass hadn't even bothered to propose. She'd dragged him into the jewelry shop after only a month of dating. He had just gone along with the engagement! How insulting was that?! He hadn't cared about a marriage to her and, she adjusted her breasts for better viewing, no one insulted her like that! No one!

Adding insult to injury, she wanted his credit card back! She needed his money! She hated living with her father, who had cut her off and, hence the engagement to Oliver, as well as moving into his gorgeous penthouse. Seriously, the man was disgustingly wealthy. Too bad he didn't know how to spend all of those delicious billions!

Desiree was very good at spending money. She'd learned at her mother's knee and was an expert at wheedling money out of men. If she'd just kept out of Oliver's bed with the gardener or landscaper or... whoever...they would be married right now.

Accepting that she'd made a serious error there, she considered her options. She wanted Oliver back. Correction, she wanted his money back. And she wanted access to his bedroom back! The man's house was gorgeous and...okay, so when he actually took the time to have sex with her, Oliver was truly exceptional. Most of the men she'd gone out with over the years would simply stick their thing in and grunt until they were finished, then grin at her as if they'd just gifted her with something beautiful.

Phhpt! Men! They had no idea how much women seriously hated sex!

At least with Oliver, she hadn't had to pull out one of her favorite toys afterwards and find that elusive release. He'd known the value of all of her various parts.

Still, it was his money she was after. The sex was fine, but she could really take it or leave it. Money though...! And the power! Good grief, being on Oliver's arm at the various events around town was even better than sex! Power was the real gem here. Power and prestige. Walking into any event with Oliver was a bit like being a rock star. Everyone wanted a minute of his time. Everyone wanted to be him or be her because she was with him. The envy from the other women was almost palpable!

Yeah, she knew all that crap about being one's own powerhouse. Blah blah blah. Whatever! Let the feminists find their power on their own. She didn't mind being the arm candy of a powerful man! In fact, she loved it! She'd planned on quitting her irritating job right after she got a wedding ring on her finger!

As she stepped back into her office and settled into the chair, she sneered at the e-mails waiting for her response. She hated working! Seriously, why did anyone prefer working to staying at home, sleeping in until it was time for a spa appointment?

Which brought her back to her original issue. How was she to get Oliver back? He didn't seem angry. He hadn't even been all that pissed when he'd found her having sex with what's his name! Which was pretty damn insulting! He'd just ordered her to leave. Then the bastard had fouled up her plans to talk some reason into him when he'd gathered up all of her stuff and sent it back to her. She'd been pretty proud of that idea, until that ridiculous box had arrived. Most of the stuff wasn't even hers! She'd just bought it and dispersed the stuff around his house, in anticipation of needing an opportunity at some point. Desiree knew that she wasn't the easiest person to keep around and had figured out little traps to keep a man humble and at her beck and call.

Unfortunately, Oliver hadn't fallen under her spell, the bastard.

So, what was going on? He'd been distracted over the past few days.

Did he have a new lover?

No. Desiree knew Oliver well enough now to know he was a picky bastard. He didn't play the bed-hopping game that had gotten her this far.

So, what was she going to do? Perhaps it was time to do a bit of investigative work, she thought with relish as she tapped her pencil against her desk. Yes, it was time to find out what Oliver was up to.

Chapter 4

Maggie hefted the casserole dish, careful to keep the hot pads underneath to protect her hands.

Opening the door to her apartment, she propped it open before walking down the concrete sidewalk to Mick's apartment. When she stood in front of it, she adjusted the casserole in her hands, then knocked using her elbow.

A moment later, Mick opened the door and she smiled. "Hey! I just fixed up your favorite."

Mick's eyes brightened as he took in the potato chip covered meal. "Macaroni and cheese?" he whispered reverently.

"Exactly!" Maggie replied, laughing softly at his excitement.

"What's the occasion?" he asked, carefully taking the casserole dish from her. "And are you going to come in and have some with me?"

Maggie peered inside the apartment, spotting Jimmy and Eddie on the sofa. They were watching sports, each with a beer in hand, except for Jimmy, who had a glass of iced tea. "Nope. I made two so I have more in my kitchen waiting for me."

Mick nodded his head. "What's the occasion?" he asked.

Maggie shrugged. "I saw you walking home from work earlier today. You looked a bit sad."

He laughed. "Eh, a customer stole his car back from me."

"Without paying?" she asked, already knowing the answer.

Mick shifted the warm casserole in his hands slightly, shrugging his skinny shoulders. "Yeah. I kinda saw it coming. I shoulda taken his car keys home with me."

Maggie put a comforting hand on his arm, shaking her head. "You should call the police, Mick. That's not right."

"I know. And maybe I will, tomorrow. But it's Debbie's uncle's car.

And you know how she's been struggling lately."

Maggie knew. Twelve year old Debbie had learning disabilities and the other kids in her class teased her cruelly. Molly had found a special tutor to help Debbie, but it was slow progress at the moment. Debbie's uncle was...well, he wasn't the worst, but that wasn't saying much.

"Yeah, I understand." If Mick called the police, they'd arrest the uncle. And the man might be slime, but he brought home a few dollars to help keep food on the table and pay the rent. Without the uncle's contribution, the family might be in serious trouble. "It's not right, but I understand why you're not going to involve the police." She smiled and waved to the men, then stepped back. "Well, I just...enjoy the mac and cheese, guys."

With that, she turned on her heel and hurried back to her apartment.

Oliver lingered by the corner of the building, not sure he had heard correctly. Maggie had made the guy dinner just because he'd had a hard day? The boxes of ceramic tiles in his arms were heavy, but Oliver continued to stand there, watching Maggie hurry back to her apartment, her hips swaying slightly with each step. He was mesmerized and painfully turned on. Not just by her walk, but by the kind gesture. She'd made dinner for a guy who'd had a bad day. Just because he'd had a bad day! She hadn't even known that he'd been robbed! She'd cooked the guy his favorite meal out of the goodness of her heart.

That was so far outside of his realm of understanding that he had trouble grasping the concept. Yeah, he donated enormous sums of money to charities every year. But he barely even acknowledged the donations. It didn't take more effort on his part other than sending a message to his accountant to make the donation happen.

"Maggie makes the *best* macaroni and cheese," Louise gushed.

Oliver jumped so hard he nearly dropped the boxes of tiles. "What?"

Louise nodded in the direction of Maggie's apartment door. "Maggie. She makes this mac and cheese concoction that is so gooey and cheesy."

"And she crumbles potato chips on top!" another voice chimed in.

Turning, he found Nora on his other side. He should have anticipated that. Where Louise was, so was Nora. The ladies might be of different ethnicities, but they were sisters in the most fundamental sort of way. It was very sweet, the way their friendship had persevered through the decades.

"And she just...made it for Mick?"

Nora nodded. "Yeah. You should have seen him this afternoon. He was pretty upset. That's why Eddie and Jimmy are with him now."

He glanced at the plate in Louise's hands. "Are those your butterscotch cookies?" he whispered, awe in his voice as his mouth started watering.

Nora chuckled. "Nah. Mick's favorite cookie is oatmeal with chocolate chips."

Oliver might have groaned at the idea of freshly baked cookies. But his attention turned back to look in Maggie's direction. "So, what do I have to do to get a taste of her mac and cheese?" he asked, a bit desperate at the idea. Of course, he wanted a taste of more than just the casserole!

Louise patted his arm, shaking her head. "You'll figure it out, honey," she said and the ladies walked down the concrete, pausing at Mick's door. They had a brief conversation with the man, handing over the precious cookies, then moved on down to their own apartments.

Oliver waited, his arms about to fall off, but he wanted to make sure that they reached their apartment safely. This apartment complex might be an oasis, but it was surrounded by some pretty rough elements.

When both ladies waved to him, letting him know that they realized what he was doing, then entered their apartments, only then did Oliver move on down to the dilapidated apartment that Maggie had allowed him to rent. There was no doubt about it. Maggie was the one who "allowed" people to reside here.

Of course, she hadn't required him to even sign a lease. Which meant that she hadn't done a background or credit check on him. Interesting, he thought as he moved towards the bathroom.

He'd already knocked out the old pink tiles from the back of the shower area and replaced the cement board. Next, he planned to glue the tiles to the board tonight. Tomorrow, once the glue had cured, he'd grout the tiles into place.

For the next several hours, he worked steadily, fixing the tiles with the pins to ensure that they were straight, all the while, wondering about Maggie. Was she seeing someone? He doubted it. He didn't think that she'd react to him the way she had last weekend if she was committed to someone else.

And what about her history? Why was she driving such an old car when she should be able to afford something newer? Why was her apartment almost completely empty? The furniture was older than she was, so was it all just hand-me-downs from relatives? If so, where were those relatives now?

It was a fascinating mystery that drew him in.

Chapter 5

Maggie picked herself up, smacking her hands together to knock the gravel off.

"Are you okay, Maggie?" Louise called out.

Maggie turned around, ignoring the blue pickup as it pulled into a parking space.

"I'm fine," she called back, waving to show her that she was uninjured.

"Good! Now stop Davie!"

Maggie swung around and, sure enough, the little boy wobbling down the parking lot was just about to ride out into the busy street.

"Davie, pump the breaks!" she yelled, sprinting down the asphalt parking lot in pursuit of the eight year old who was just learning to ride his bike.

"I can't!" Davie yelled. She heard the panic in his voice and made her legs go faster. "I don't know how!"

Darn it! Davie had asked if she could teach him how to ride and he'd tumbled about ten times over the past hour. This was the furthest he'd managed to go without falling over and...good grief, he was about to turn into road pizza!

Suddenly, someone grabbed the boy off the bike, pulling him into his arms. A moment later, the bike hit the ground.

Maggie skidded to a stop, her hand coming to her throat as she looked up into the eyes of Oliver, who carried Davie back to the safety of the sidewalk.

"I'm sorry!" Maggie gasped. "Are you okay?"

Davie was grinning from ear to ear, thrilled with his progress. "I did it!" he yelled excitedly. "Did you see how far I went, Maggie? Did you see me?"

Maggie nodded, trying to calm her racing heart. "Yeah. I saw! You did a great job!" She reached up to ruffle his hair affectionately, pretending that she wasn't a little faint after such a scare.

"Let's do it again!" he announced, wiggling out of Oliver's arms as he raced back to retrieve his bike. Thankfully, he turned it around so that he was heading towards the other side of the parking lot in front of the apartment buildings. At the other end was a hedge made up of benign boxwood hedges, so if he ran into them, he'd only get scraped up.

"Maybe we should practice using the brakes before you get back on, Davie," she suggested delicately.

He grinned and his white teeth sparkled in the early dusk light. "I'll figure it out. I'm an expert now."

Maggie laughed, but she wasn't overly amused. It was more a laugh of relief than humor.

"He's going to kill himself, isn't he?" Oliver commented, standing next to Maggie with his hands on his hips as they both watched the boy wobble off. But he made it all the way to the hedge. And thankfully for her plants, he did figure out the brakes.

Molly nodded somberly. "Yeah, probably. But he's going to have fun doing it."

"Why are you teaching him how to ride his bike? Where are his parents?"

"Well, his mother works nights as a receptionist at the health clinic down the street. So, she can't be here in the evenings. She'll work until about nine o'clock, but then has to clean up. Louise watches him in the afternoon, along with several of the other neighborhood kids down at the Center in the after school program. They get their homework done during that time period, then there are organized games and such. The parents pick up the kids after that."

She knew that she was rambling, but the way he was looking at her made her nervous.

That was a stupid thought. Anything he did made her nervous. So, his gaze only intensified her anxiety.

"That doesn't answer my question," he replied softly.

She glanced up at him, but kept her gaze on Davie.

"His mother doesn't know how to ride a bike," she admitted.

"And his father?"

She shrugged. "He's gone."

"That's pretty tragic," he replied.

Another dismissive shrug. "It happens."

Oliver looked at her again, this time, his gaze was assessing. "Your father disappeared as well?"

There was a long pause, but she eventually nodded. "Right after I was born," she admitted. "I'm from Texas, originally," she explained, unable to hide the pride in her voice. "Texas is a beautiful state, but we're still a bit old fashioned and believe that a mother and father should be married when a child is brought into the world." She took several slow, deep breaths, releasing the pain that came every time she talked about her family. "In my case, neither my mother nor my father decided to stick around."

"What happened?" he asked.

She knew that she should have kept her mouth shut. But because she was nervous around this man with his wide, strong shoulders, and that chest that just begged for a woman to lay her cheek against, Maggie admitted that she was weak. Weak and pathetic when he spoke to her. She did silly things, like admit her tragic past.

"My father skedaddled right after my birth. Then my mother...well, apparently, I was a tough baby to bring into this world and my mother was a delicate little thing. She died shortly after my birth." Maggie swallowed, forcing her lips into a smile. "But I had my grandmother. She was always there for me."

Oliver's eyes narrowed and Maggie knew that she'd revealed too much. "What's in the bag?" she asked, trying to change the subject.

Oliver glanced down, having forgotten the bag entirely. "Oh...just something for my apartment," he said, not mentioning that this was the new grout for the bathroom. The tiles should have set by now. The grout would give a whole new air to the place. He'd start on the floors next.

"Is everything okay?" she asked. "I mean, I know that the renovation teams are hard at work in the other apartments so as soon as they are ready, you can move into one. And if there's something that isn't working, just let me know. If I can't fix it, I know that Mick or Eddie, or one of the others, can. No need to suffer with broken things. I know that the décor leaves a lot to be desired, but when I checked that apartment, everything seemed to work properly."

He smiled and that look stunned her enough that she finally stopped talking.

"Everything is working perfectly," he assured her.

She snorted and he chuckled. "Okay, I'll admit that the cabinets need some work. So, I just took them down and stored stuff on shelves."

She nodded. "Yeah, that's what I did when I moved in as well. The manager's office was pretty bad before. The previous manager was disgusting!"

"Why haven't *you* moved into one of the renovated places?"

Oliver watched the emotions flit over her features. There was another mystery, he realized.

She waved her hand in the air. "Oh, there are others who need a decent place to live more than I do. There are so many families that just need a little help."

"You don't think that you need a break?" he asked softly.

She laughed. "Oh, I had a pretty good childhood. It's my turn to sacrifice for a while." She turned and watched as Davie maneuvered around the empty parking spaces. "You're doing a great job, Davie!" she called encouragingly.

"He learned pretty fast."

"Davie is a good kid. His mother is studying to become a nurse practitioner."

"Why not a doctor?" he asked.

Another snort. "Because medical school is expensive. Barbara is only able to take one class per semester. With her two jobs, plus Davie, plus that one class, she's pretty tied up."

"I didn't realize," he said, feeling like a jerk for being so insensitive. The people he knew who went to medical school had their parents pay for the whole thing. They were smart people, but they didn't have to worry about financial issues.

"Where are you from?" she asked, squinting up at him.

He laughed. "I grew up right here in Virginia. My family still lives in Richmond. I went to the University of Virginia for both my undergraduate and graduate degrees." He paused, realizing that he might have made a mistake in admitting that much. If Maggie thought he wasn't a worthy candidate for the apartment, would she kick him out? He didn't want to leave until he understood Maggie better. She was a mystery. A fascinating, beautiful mystery. Once he understood her better, he'd get out of the apartment and make room for someone who actually needed it. Until he understood why she did the things she did, he wanted to stick around.

"Maggie!" Louise called from the sidewalk.

"What's up?" Maggie called, glancing over at Davie to make sure he was still upright.

"Jimmy needs ya!"

Maggie turned to look up at Oliver. "Will you keep an eye on Davie for me?"

Oliver nodded and waved her off. "Sure. Go."

Oliver stood there, the grout still in the bag in his arms as Davie rolled slowly over, stopping next to him.

"Man, you've got it bad," the boy teased, shaking his head as he rode off, still wobbly but better than before.

Oliver sighed and put the grout back in the bed of his pickup, then, pushing the sleeves up on his shirt, he followed after Davie to give him a few more tips.

Chapter 6

Oliver checked his cell phone as he hurried out of the apartment. He had meetings in an hour and he still needed to head back to his place to shower and change. He could do that here, but Oliver was still hiding his identity and his job by wearing jeans and a tee shirt. Sometimes, he felt like a fraud. But other times, he revived his flagging sense of right and wrong by doing something kind for the people who lived here. For instance, he'd ordered his security team to figure out who had stolen back their car from Mick's repair shop without paying, then had "gently encouraged" the man to pay Mick the money he'd owed him. Not by physical violence, but his security team had shown the guy the evidence of his transgressions and promised to bring that evidence to the police.

The next day, Mick had come home shaking his head in disbelief, muttering about strange happenings. Oliver took that to mean that the guy had paid up. Plus, he was secretly renovating the apartment, paying for the supplies himself. He'd also gotten his assistant to research scholarship opportunities for Davie's mother. Since most of the scholarship deadlines for the year had passed, Oliver ended up setting up a scholarship fund through his company, anonymously, of course. Then his assistant had worked through that system to apply that scholarship money to Davie's mother's school tuition.

Davie was grinning from ear to ear, excited for his mother.

That had felt good.

What hadn't felt good was not seeing Maggie for the past several days. Was she hiding from him? Had he offended her somehow?

Damn, he needed to see her! He just needed a smile from her to make his day brighter.

But that wasn't going to happen, he realized. And when he came around the corner of the building, he realized that his day was about to get even worse. His truck, the beat up old truck that he'd bought as part of his disguise, was open. The engine hood propped up and...was someone actually stealing his truck engine right here in middle of the parking lot? Seriously?!

But as he approached, the hood slammed closed and Mick straightened up, cleaning a wrench with an oily rag.

"Mick?" Oliver called out, startling the man into looking up. "What were you doing to my truck?" he asked, trying not to sound suspicious but...well, hell, he was suspicious!

"Your timing belt was off. That clicking sound? The belt was fixing to break."

Oliver blinked at the elderly man for a long moment. "It...was?" he finally asked, stunned.

"Yeah. It's fixed now." Mick collected his toolbox and his cooler filled with his lunch supplies.

Oliver watched as the elderly man headed towards his shop, not sure what to say. "How much do I owe you?" he asked, because that's what any other person would ask, right?

Wrong!

Mick turned back, frowning at Oliver for a long moment. "If you see Jimmy at the ABC store," he started off, referring to the alcohol beverage center, the only stores with licenses to sell hard alcohol in Virginia, "stop and talk to him. *Don't* pass him by."

Then Mick quietly turned and headed off. There wasn't much traffic this early in the morning. It was relatively quiet now, but soon, the traffic would be whizzing by, the sun would come up, and the world would once again speed through the day.

Which is exactly what Oliver should be doing. Instead, he stood there, watching the elderly man who was walking down the same street towards the same job that he'd been doing for decades.

When Mick was out of sight, Oliver turned and looked at his truck once again. Then back at the apartment buildings. More specifically, Maggie's windows. He wanted to go to her, to talk to her. Just smile at her. Instead, he got into his truck and drove away.

Maggie watched as Oliver's pickup drove smoothly out of the parking lot. She'd watched him this morning. She'd seen the confused look on his handsome features and wanted to laugh. She understood that confusion. Maggie had been confused when she'd first arrived at Rose Garden Apartments. It was a world away from the norm, she thought.

Turning away from the window now that Oliver had gone, she picked up her notebook and got on with her day. She had lots to do.

Chapter 7

"We have a major problem!" Molly announced as the others gathered at the Center.

Lilly Gataki waddled over to the group of chairs that Molly had arranged, groaning when she spotted the overstuffed recliner. "I'm *not* sitting there!" she declared, grumbling under her breath.

Jimmy glared at her. "Woman, you are too pregnant to be this stubborn," and he took her hands. "If you won't do it for me, do it for your baby. She needs rest."

Lilly glared up at the former Navy SEAL, but he was even more stubborn than she. With a resigned sigh, she allowed him to lower her into the chair. "I feel like a beached whale," she grumbled.

"You look like one too," Louise agreed cheerfully as she stepped into the circle and sat down on a folding chair. "But a *beautiful* beached whale." She patted Lilly's hand and grinned.

Lilly glared at her friend. "You're not my favorite anymore," she decided.

Nora came around on Lilly's other side, handing her a small plate of cookies. "That's because *I'm* your favorite, right?" she asked.

Lilly sighed with happiness as she took a bite of a cookie. "Absolutely!"

Jimmy shook his head, and grabbed an apple from one of the tables. With surprising speed, he swiped the plate of cookies and replaced them with the apple. "The baby needs vitamins." He turned to glare at Nora. "Not sugar." He walked to the opposite side of the circle, scarfing down the cookies as he went.

Lilly knew he was right, but her mouth watered for another cookie anyway. Unfortunately, Jimmy was too far away for her to steal them back. Plus, Molly snuck around behind the chair and, with a flip of the side switch, swooped Lilly's feet into the air with the footrest. That meant that there wasn't much she could do about retrieving her stolen cookies. Jimmy knew it and snickered as he ate another one.

Thankfully, Eddie came around and snatched the plate, taking the last two cookies and gobbling them up. He turned to Lilly and gave her a wink, as if he were somehow conspiring with her against Jimmy.

Not so much, Lilly thought miserably as she took a bite of the apple. It was sweet and delicious and much healthier. But those were Nora's cranberry walnut cookies! She loved how the sweetness of the cookie as well as the contrast with the tart cranberries. Besides, Jimmy didn't even *like* nuts in his cookies!

"The walnuts are good for arteries," she mumbled around a bite of apple.

Molly sat down next to Mick. "Can we get down to the urgent reason I called us together?" she asked, looking around with a look that informed everyone that she would not be delayed any longer.

"What's up?" Lilly asked, shifting so that she was more comfortable. As embarrassing as she found the chair, it was incredibly comfortable. Plus, the elevated footrest definitely helped with her swollen ankles. Just a few more months, she promised, patting her belly as she took another bite of the apple.

"The problem is that our plan isn't working. We need to be more actively pushing Maggie and Oliver together."

"I thought that he'd moved into one of the apartments?" Lilly asked, looking around. "Maggie always helps with the renovations. They should be together all the time then, right?"

"That's true," Molly explained. "But from what I can figure out, Oliver is doing it all himself during the evening hours. Maggie is working on the renovations with the teams during the day. She doesn't venture anywhere near Oliver's apartment. So, we need to up the stakes if we're going to get these two together."

Louise nodded her head. "Seems to me that all those two do is watch each other from a distance. No action."

"Oliver is trying to be a gentleman," Nora sniffed.

"Yeah, I agree," Eddie put in. "But this is Maggie we're talking about. And in the year that she's been here with us, she hasn't shown interest in anyone we've brought around. But the moment she saw Oliver, she was smitten."

"And he's just as head over heels with her," Molly agreed. "But something is holding him back."

"It's Maggie," Nora announced. "She's always running away from him."

"Texas!" Mick snorted. "Something happened to her in Texas and now she's afraid of her own shadow."

"She only gets nervous around Oliver," Louise pointed out.

Everyone in the group nodded, except for Lilly. "Who is this Oliver guy? I don't know about him."

"He's a construction worker that showed up looking for a place to live. Maggie thinks he's ex-military."

"But he's not," Jimmy countered.

No one argued as Molly continued. "She gave him the apartment four doors down from hers. But he's a mystery."

"Should someone do a background check on him?"

Jimmy shook his head. "He's fine. I've already looked into him."

There was a brief silence as that news was absorbed. No one doubted him though. The former Navy SEAL was coming back to life with a vengeance.

"Okay, so Oliver is a good guy. But Maggie is running away from him. What's our plan to get them together?" Molly asked, looking around the small group of friends and co-conspirators.

"Soccer!" Lilly blurted.

Everyone turned in her direction, not sure if her outburst was a symptom of her pregnancy or a solution.

"Soccer!" she repeated when their blank looks continued. "Maggie took over the girls' soccer team last year. Soccer is about to start again now that school is back in session."

Eddie nodded, chuckling. "She asked if I could help her coach the team!" he announced, leaning forward.

Slow smiles lit up every face. "You're going to ask Oliver if he would fill in for you, aren't you?" Nora asked, grinning mischievously.

"Damn straight I am," he agreed as he theatrically clutched his back. "I'm feeling a bit of sciatica coming on." He added a slight groan for effect.

"Excellent!" Molly replied, clapping her hands. "Okay, what else?"

"Isn't the community garden harvest coming up next weekend?" Louise offered.

"Sure is," Molly laughed.

"And we need a few more volunteers, don't we?" Lilly asked.

Molly jumped up and grabbed a big piece of paper from her desk. "That's a good idea. I'm working out the assignments now. I can make sure Oliver and Maggie are stationed in the same area. Maggie wouldn't dare leave until everything is done, which will give Oliver a chance to make his case."

"Okay, what else?" Molly asked, scribbling frantically.

For the next hour, the group brainstormed. By the time they walked back out into the gorgeous autumn afternoon, the plans were in place. It was ingenious!

Chapter 8

"Okay ladies! Gather round and let's talk about–" Maggie paused as she watched a man in well-worn jeans and yet another faded tee shirt climb out of his pickup. "What's he doing here?" Maggie asked, startled when Oliver reached into the back of his truck and pulled out a mesh bag filled with...glory be! New soccer balls!

Almost in unison, the girls gasped as they watched the man toss the bag of pretty, shiny soccer balls over his shoulder and pulled out a second bag. What this bag might contain was a mystery that had all fifteen girls, as well as their now-stammering coach, gawking in wonder and anticipation.

"Hello ladies," Oliver said as he dropped both bags on the grass. He turned to Maggie to explain, "Eddie caught me on my way to work this morning. He said something happened to his back and asked if I could help you with soccer practice." He looked at the girls who were all examining the mesh bag filled with soccer balls. "I hope you don't mind me helping out as a substitute assistant coach until he feels better?"

Maggie's eyes narrowed suspiciously. "He seemed okay earlier, when I saw him carrying a bag of grout up to the second story apartments," she muttered. Then sighed and shook her head. "But yes, thank you for filling in. I think the real reason Eddie bailed on me is because he doesn't know how to play soccer. He helped me last year but never really understood what off-sides meant."

"The company I'm currently working for donates sports equipment for local teams. When I mentioned that I was stepping in to help, I was offered a stipend to buy some equipment."

Maggie gasped, her eyes dropping to the filled bags. "You mean, all of this is ours to *keep*?"

The girls had opened the other bag and were pulling out mesh jerseys.

43

Half of the girls would wear the mesh shirts over their tee shirts and the other half wouldn't. That made it easier to identify one's opponent.

"Sure. The owner is a pretty good guy."

One of the girls pulled out a stack of small, orange cones. "What are these for?" she asked, wrinkling her nose.

"Those are to run drills," Oliver explained, and glanced at Maggie as if that should have been just a standard piece of equipment.

"We run drills around sticks," she explained with a shrug.

"Not anymore," he announced. Then he looked down at the thoroughly beaten up, filthy soccer ball resting at Maggie's feet. "Where are the others?"

She laughed, toeing the ball. "This is it," she explained. "We've gotten by with one ball so far. But," she looked down at the other bag filled with pristine, beautiful soccer balls, "we'll definitely make use of those!"

He laughed and dumped the balls out onto the ground. He looked around, squinting in the setting sun. "*This* is the practice field?"

Maggie chuckled again. "Practice and game field. We share the field on the weekends with the other neighborhood sports teams."

Oliver's lips compressed and she looked around with a shrug. "It's not so bad," she said. "It's big and open, so no one will get hurt. Plus, it's so filled with weeds, that we don't have to fight for space like we would if we lived in the suburbs and had nicer fields."

"Right," he sighed. "So, what's the first drill?"

Maggie picked up her clipboard and started calling out names, separating the girls into squads. They did several drills; altering the practice now that there were so many soccer balls to use. For the next ninety minutes, Maggie took half of the team while Oliver worked with the other half. She taught defensive skills and Oliver worked on offense. When the practice was over, the girls were exhausted, but also exhilarated. As they left the field, collecting orange cones and soccer balls as they went, they were laughing and smiling, high fiving each other as they talked eagerly about the next practice.

In a sudden panic, Maggie watched as the girls waved goodbye, leaving Maggie standing beside Oliver with the equipment at their feet.

"You look tired," he commented.

Maggie glanced up at Oliver, feeling that strange swooping sensation in her stomach that always happened when she was close to him. Hence, why she stayed away from him.

"It's been a long day," she replied.

"I'll walk you home," he teased, since they lived in the same building.

She laughed, but he could see the blush on her cheeks and loved it.

He grabbed both bags, tossing them over his shoulder. They weren't heavy, but he liked walking beside her with them in one hand and Maggie on the other side. He'd like to reach out and touch her hand, weave his fingers through hers. That was such an old-fashioned idea that he mentally rolled his eyes.

"What's so funny?" she asked, walking alongside him as she kicked the taller weeds out of her way.

He sighed and looked out at the parking lot. "I was just wondering how long it has been since I held a woman's hand. Then I realized that I don't think I've ever held a woman's hand."

She stopped and looked up at him. "Never?"

He shook his head, chuckling now. "Nope. I was an arrogant bastard in high school. Didn't really have a girlfriend. So any time I walked with a girl, it was for an ulterior reason."

"You...want to hold my hand?" she asked, seeming to almost choke over the words.

He stopped and turned to look down at her. "Yeah. I'd really like to get to know you, Maggie." He moved closer. "I don't want to pressure you. But you...fascinate me. There's something about you that pulls me in, but the look in your eyes tells me to stay the hell away." His hand reached up, touching her cheek lightly. "I'm not sure which message to listen to."

There was a long silence as she gazed into his eyes. "I'm not sure either," she replied honestly.

He smiled, but pulled back. "How about if you just let me get to know you?" he offered. "No pressure." He took her hand and laced his fingers with hers. "I suspect that you've had a bad relationship in the past." He rubbed his thumb over hers. "So have I. I don't trust women easily, but..." he sighed and looked thoughtfully up at the darkening sky. "I'd like to trust you, Maggie. If you'd let me in enough to get to know you." He saw the wariness in her eyes. "But if you need more time, that's fine. Like I said, I won't pressure you."

Maggie opened her mouth to respond, but the words wouldn't form. Thoughts flew from her mind. Oliver wanted...her? How...shockingly wonderful!

"Well, I guess—"

"Don't answer me now," he replied quickly. "Why don't we drive home and you can sleep on it?"

She smiled, thinking that she could answer him immediately. "Okay, if you *want* to wait for my answer, then that sounds like a plan."

With that, she turned on her heel and headed for his truck, leaving Oliver standing in the field looking flummoxed.

A moment later, he pulled his head out of his ass and hurried forward.

"Wait a minute," he ordered, touching her arm. "Would you...?"

"Yes," she replied, then slipped her hand into his and started walking again. When he stood there, still trying to understand, she tugged, getting his feet moving again.

"Drive me home, Oliver," she ordered playfully as she stepped into his truck.

Oliver tossed the equipment into the back, fighting back the triumphant smile that would probably make him look like an overly eager school boy. Pulling himself into the truck, he started it up and backed out of the parking space. But before he pulled into traffic, he looked over at her. "Does that mean that you'll make me your famous macaroni and cheese?" he asked, hope practically dripping from his tone.

Maggie cracked up and Oliver thought her laughter was the most beautiful sound he'd ever heard.

"Oh no!" she argued. "You'll have to do something pretty extraordinary for that!"

"Fair enough. Will you let me buy you pizza then?"

She thought about it for perhaps a half second. "Yes. That would be really nice. But you're not buying me dinner. We'll split the cost," she declared.

He stared at her for a long moment, then shook his head. "Maggie, the things that...well, never mind. Let's get some pizza." And with that, he pulled into traffic, grinning as he drove to the pizza place a few blocks away, where they laughed and talked about nothing in particular as they gorged on pizza.

When he walked her to her door that night, Oliver hesitated. Another first for him. But when Maggie looked up into his eyes, he knew what he had to do. Leaning forward, he brushed his lips against hers, lightly, then pulled back.

"Thank you for a lovely evening, Maggie," he told her softly. Then he walked away.

Oliver couldn't believe it, but as he shut the door on his own apartment, he knew that walking away that night was the perfect ending to a perfect evening. Never in his life had he thought that walking away from a beautiful woman would be perfect, but he didn't want to pressure Maggie into a sexual relationship too quickly. This was too important. *She* was too important!

Chapter 9

Maggie was going insane. That was the only possible explanation for what was going on inside her head. She couldn't sleep, ate way too many cookies, and her brain felt as if it were spinning out of control.

Oliver was always around! He was with her during their soccer practices on Tuesday and Thursday nights, and after every game, he walked her home, leaving her on her doorstep with a gentle kiss when he lifted her hand to his lips. On Saturday morning, he showed up at the community garden. He dug up potatoes, beets, and carrots. He plucked apples out of the tree faster than anyone else. He even hauled the harvest to the Center and helped cook it up and distribute to the neighborhood residents. That was *her* thing! She loved handing out the bags of whatever was harvested that day, feeling as if she were accepting gifts from the earth and sharing them with the world.

But Maggie couldn't ask him to stop. When Oliver was there, people laughed. He was charming and funny. He got down on his knees and played tic-tac-toe with chalk on the asphalt, then joined in an impromptu soccer game with the teens. Oliver sat with the seniors and listened to their stories. Really listened! She even stopped by the nursery one morning and caught him with three toddlers piled into his lap, reading them stories, patiently re-reading the pages whenever the children asked.

Yep. It was insanity, she told herself. There was no other explanation for what was going on in her mind. Every moment of the day, she thought about him. And there was no place for her to hide. He'd invaded her normal hiding places and it made her dizzy with...hope?

No, that was impossible. She'd lost any kind of hope the day she'd left Texas so long ago.

Hope was a pointless emotion, she reminded herself as she carried her basket of dirty clothes to the laundry room. Hope was a waste of time.

Shoving the heavy metal door open, she sighed as she...came to a complete stop.

"Damn it!" she muttered when she spotted Oliver standing beside a dryer, about to put laundry detergent onto his dirty clothes. Goodness, he looked adorable holding up the detergent bottle to the light so he could read the instructions.

Maggie shook her head. "Just walk away," she whispered to herself.

He must have heard her mumbling because he jumped slightly and those amazing blue eyes of his narrowed in on her standing there in the doorway. Immediately, she knew she'd lost her chance for a strategic retreat. It was obvious that she was holding a ton of dirty clothes. So if she backed away now, he'd know that she was a chicken.

Self-preservation was a funny thing, she thought. Then she realized what he was about to do and...!

"Don't!" she yelped when Oliver measured out the laundry detergent and his hand headed towards the dryer opening.

"Don't put laundry detergent in?"

She laughed at his confused expression.

"Correct. That would be a bad idea," she replied, stepping all the way into the laundry room. Of course, it was Monday night and most of the other residents would have done their laundry over the weekend. Which was why she normally did her laundry on Monday, to free up the washers and dryers for others.

"Why wouldn't I put the laundry detergent in now? Should I put it in later?"

Maggie couldn't hide her amusement. He was so cute! In a sexy, overly muscular, alpha male sort of way. His arms and shoulders pulled the material of his tee shirt tight over the muscles and his stomach was impressively flat. The jeans he wore looked...amazing on his long, muscular legs and...well, there was just something inherently sexy about a man doing laundry, she thought. That might be weird, but in Maggie's mind, it was hot!

"Well, yes. You definitely need to put laundry detergent into the washing machine."

"So...what's the problem?"

She dumped her heavy basket on the table. "That's the dryer. Not the washing machine."

He frowned at the large, metal machine, then down at the laundry detergent. After a moment, he shook his head and sighed. "Obviously, I'm new at this."

She laughed again. "Yeah, I get that," she told him. "Since I was in the same situation not too long ago, I'll take pity on you and give you some pointers." She walked over to the line of washers. "These are the washing machines." She pointed to the line next to him. "Those are dryers. If you put the laundry detergent onto your clothes, then turn on that machine, you'll simply cook the detergent into your clothes and make an even bigger mess."

Maggie knew that she was in big trouble when he grinned. Darn it, a man who could laugh at himself was dangerous!

"Okay, excellent tip! Put the clothes into the correct machine first."

With that, he grabbed his laundry basket and started loading his clothes back in. "So, is there a trick to the washing machine?" he asked.

She laughed, unable to hide her amusement at what should be a normal task for any adult.

"Well, the first thing you do is sort the clothes," she explained, waving for him to bring his laundry over to the washing machine. She pointed to the washer next to hers. Oliver and she started loading clothes into the machines. "It looks like most of your dirty clothes are jeans, so I'd recommend that you do those separately. When there are multiple machines available, it's easier to get multiple loads done quickly."

He stuffed his jeans into the washing machine, watching as Maggie sorted her jeans as well. "My jeans don't fill up this washer. Why don't you put your jeans in here with mine?" he suggested.

Maggie froze, startled by his suggestion. She looked up at him, holding a pair of her well-worn jeans above a separate washing machine.

Since she was still stunned by his offer, he took the pair of jeans from her and stuffed them into the washer. "We'll save time and money doing it this way," he explained, and reached around her to grab the other pairs of jeans from her laundry basket.

As he did that, Maggie held her breath, realizing that she was literally cocooned by his body, his chest pressing against her back, his arms surrounding her in the most delightful, wonderful, dangerous way. She stifled a moan of desire as she gripped the washing machine tightly and closed her eyes, waiting for him to finish collecting her jeans.

Maggie wanted to tell him that they should do separate loads, but she could barely think, much less breathe or form coherent words.

"Are you okay, Maggie?" he asked softly, his breath brushing tantalizingly over the sensitive shell of her ear.

"I'm fine!" she squeaked.

His chest pressed more firmly against her back, so close that she could easily feel his muscles flex as he grabbed the last pair of jeans.

"Yes, you are," he said, kissing the top of her head.

When he was back in front of the fully loaded washer, she took a slow, deep, shaky breath, trying to bring herself back to "normal".

"Um…" she blinked, trying to remember the next step in the clothes-washing process. She glanced over at the washing machine filled with jeans and took another slow, deep breath.

"Does that help?" he asked.

Maggie inhaled sharply when she saw the intensity in his eyes. Good grief, he was feeling it too!

"Detergent," she whispered.

Never in her life had washing dirty clothes been an erotic experience!

"How much?" he asked, lifting his jug of detergent.

Blinking again to try to center her thoughts, she breathed in and out. Oliver was just…doing laundry. Right?

"Maggie?" he prompted.

"Hmmm?" she asked, noticing the light circle of golden yellow around his blue irises.

He moved closer. "How much laundry detergent should I use?" he asked, his voice low and husky and incredibly sexy. How in the world could a question about laundry detergent come out sounding like a caress? It was almost as if the man was asking her how much she wanted him to kiss her!

A lot, would have been her answer.

"Um…" she breathed in and out again. "For a full load, measure up to the line on the laundry detergent cap."

Maggie's attention was captured by his long, tanned fingers as he tilted the cup and the laundry detergent bottle slightly, trying to see a barely visible line.

"Got it," he said, nodding as he poured the detergent. "Just pour it in?"

"Well, sort of…drizzle it around," she explained. "So it is evenly distributed."

He did so and closed the lid. "Okay, now what?" he asked.

"Move back," she ordered. "I'll show you what to do next, but I can't have you close to me."

"Why not?" he asked, but he scooted over a few inches.

She reached over and pressed the buttons. "Because my mind…" She sighed, and tried again. "Well, never mind." She took her credit card out of her back pocket and pressed several more buttons. "There. All set."

When she turned around, he was right there! He reached out and held her still, pressing her lightly back against the vibrating machine.

"What's next?" Oliver asked. But he didn't wait for her next instruction. Instead, he kissed her, his lips brushing back and forth over hers, caressing her. Teasing her. Taunting her lips until she let out a shaky breath and kissed him back.

His hand lifted, gently cradling her head as he deepened the kiss further. Maggie opened her mouth, wanting to taste him, to feel him more
intimately. Unconsciously, she moved her body closer, pressing against
him and feeling his body respond.

"Damn, Maggie!" Oliver groaned, lifting her up so that she was sitting
on the washing machine now. With deft hands, he pressed her legs
wide and pushed his hips against hers. Maggie gasped at the intimate
contact, shocked for a moment and she pulled back, staring into his
eyes.

"Do you want me to stop?" he asked, his eyes heated as his hands slid
up her jean-clad thighs.

Maggie knew she should tell him yes. So why did "No!" come out
of her mouth? It was the wrong word, she told herself. But then her
hands slid up his arms, her fingertips testing the hard planes and edges
of his muscles. "Don't stop!" she whispered frantically as her legs
curled around his hips, pulling him in closer.

Oliver's response was to cup her bottom and pull her in even closer.
The pressure angled her body backwards ever so slightly and the pressure was even more intense!

Then he was kissing her again. His mouth was hard, his tongue soft,
his fingers sliding under her tee-shirt as he explored her body. Maggie couldn't seem to stop making strange noises, nor could she stop
her own fingers from moving along his body. She wanted him naked
and that was strange because she normally didn't like the naked male
body. Oliver was just...different. He fascinated her. Or maybe it was
simply the fact that his mouth, now moving along her neck, and his
hands, sliding higher against her ribs, caused her mind to stop thinking.
She couldn't focus on anything other than touching him and pressing
herself against him, needing his fingers to touch her more, higher! She
needed his hands on her breasts!

"I'm going to...!"

"Sorry!" a different voice gasped in surprise.

Maggie jerked away and Oliver groaned as both of them looked over
at the doorway to the laundry room.

"I'm sorry!" Molly called out again, her head turned away as she
backed up, trying to get out of the area.

"Molly stop!" Maggie called out to her friend.

"No no!" Molly replied, balancing her laundry basket on her hip with
one hand while holding her other out to stop them as she backed up
another step. "I'm leaving! Please...continue!"

Maggie pressed her hands against Oliver's shoulders, nudging him
backwards a bit. "Molly, we're leaving!" she assured her. Taking Oli-

ver's hand, Maggie tugged him towards the door where Molly stood, frozen and obviously uncomfortable, trying to keep her eyes down on the floor. "Our laundry is in the washing machines. The others are all free. You go ahead and...do your laundry. We'll just..."

Oliver was tugging her now, his fingers clasping her hand as he led her out of the laundry room. "All yours," he told Molly a moment before he pulled Maggie out into the sunshine.

Once outside, Maggie stared up at Oliver. Unfortunately, she couldn't stop the laughter as it burst out of her. She tried to cover her mouth with her hand, but Oliver was growling, tugging her down the sidewalk towards her apartment.

"This isn't funny," he warned. "I'm in pain and you're laughing at me."

Maggie followed, almost running to keep up with him. "I'm not laughing at you, Oliver," she promised him. "I'm laughing at the situation. I mean, of all of the places for a romantic interlude, the laundry room would have been the last option on my list."

"Oh yeah?" he asked, turning around and sliding his fingers into the pockets of her jeans, causing Maggie to gasp in surprise. "What would be the top option?" He unlocked the door to her apartment, pushed it open and tugged her inside.

"My top choice would be...!"

Oliver didn't give her a chance to answer him. He covered her mouth with his and kissed her again, pressing her back against the wall as his hands returned to her stomach, but this time, he didn't hesitate. His hands slid higher, cupping her breasts while his thumb ravaged her taut nipple.

All thoughts of romantic scenes disappeared as lust overwhelmed her. She lifted up onto her toes, needing to wrap her legs around him, needing to feel that pressure against her core again. Instead, she felt his hands leave her breasts and she whimpered, her fingers tugging at his shirt. She wanted it off. She wanted all of his clothes gone!

But then she felt his hands sliding against her bottom, his bare palms cupping her naked bottom. She didn't have the brain capacity to figure that out, but she groaned when he lifted her into his arms. Amazingly, her jeans and panties were gone. Another time, she might wonder about how that had happened, but right now, she needed that pressure back. Pressing her hips against his, she wiggled until she could feel that erection, then sighed with happiness when she found it.

"You're killing me, Maggie!" he growled, pulling his shirt off and dumping it onto the floor.

Were they moving? She couldn't tell because he was nibbling on her neck. Yes, they must be moving because every step he took shifted that lovely, wonderful, impressive erection against her core.

"We need to slow down, Maggie!" he growled, but a moment later, her tee-shirt almost ripped when he pulled it over her head. A fraction of a second later, his mouth latched onto her nipple and Maggie almost screamed!

"Don't slow...down!" she gasped out, her hands moving over his back, wishing he'd get his damn pants off! "You're not naked!"

He laughed softly, but stood up and pushed his jeans and boxer briefs down, then stood up, gloriously naked and Maggie's mouth fell open as she stared at him. He started to move towards her, but then he stopped.

"What's wrong?"

He shook his head as he bent to grab his jeans once more. "Nothing. Stay there!" he ordered as he pulled a condom out of his pocket.

"Just one?"

He laughed as he tore open the foil, rolling the condom down over his erection. "I have more," he promised her.

Maggie bit her lip, wanting to reach out to touch him. She must have done that because the next thing she knew, he took her hands in his and pressed her back against the mattress. "Now where were we?" he asked, his knees pressing her legs wider as his hips moved between hers.

Maggie wanted to laugh, but that firm part of him was nudging at her opening. She wanted so badly to take him in her hands and...and do something! But she couldn't seem to slow down!

"I can't...!" Oliver groaned, but he didn't finish that sentence. Instead, he thrust into her, hissing as her inner muscles clamped around his shaft. "Damn, Maggie!" His eyes closed as his head went back, but then he looked down at her, his eyes meeting hers as he waited for her body to adjust to his size. "Tell me you're okay!" he almost roared. "Tell me I didn't just hurt you!"

Maggie might have laughed, but her brain couldn't send that message to her facial muscles. Every part of her mind and body focused on the delicious feeling of him being a part of her. "You...didn't!" she gasped out, wiggling her hips in a desperate effort to get him to move. "But I'm going to hurt you if you don't...!" He moved! Oh dear heaven! The sensation of his body thrusting into hers once again was better than chocolate! It was better than ice cream!

"Oliv..." She couldn't even finish speaking his name because he thrust again. And again!

Before she could slow anything down, Maggie felt the first tremors of a climax, her eyes wide as she gripped Oliver's shoulders, unaware of her nails digging into his skin.

"I've got you," he told her. Those words were the reassurance that she hadn't known that she needed. With a strangled sound, she arched her back as a climax convulsed over her body and Maggie might have screamed, she might have been silent. She wasn't sure. It was all just so...amazing! And even that word didn't do this experience justice.

A moment later, Oliver thrust into her again and again, then froze for another moment before he shook with his own release. For several seconds, he froze over her, then he collapsed down on top of Maggie. A split second later, he groaned and shifted, pulling her with him as they exchanged positions, still intimately connected.

"Damn, Maggie!" he groaned as both of them tried to get their breathing back under control.

Maggie tried to shift. She tried to just pull away from him. But it was too hard and, in the end, she simply lay against him, limp and completely zoned out.

Chapter 10

The knocking was really annoying! Oliver rolled over, fully intending to ignore whoever was rude enough to pound on the door at...he
cracked his eyes far enough open to look at the time...eight o'clock in
the morning. No one who arrived before nine o'clock was significant
enough to worry about. More importantly, anyone who arrived unan-
nounced should be shot. Or at least stopped by his doorman.

Rolling over, he pulled the pillow close, intending to go back to sleep.
But when he pulled the pillow close, he realized that the pillow wasn't
who he really wanted to pull close.

He looked around. "Where the hell are you?" he asked of the empty
room. Unfortunately, a reply wasn't forthcoming. Maggie was gone!

That woke him up a bit more. The banging was becoming more
impatient. There was shouting now, on top of the pounding. Rubbing
a hand over his face, he sighed and dropped his feet to the floor. A
cursory look around revealed his jeans, in a heap, right where he'd left
them. Right next to Maggie's purple panties, he noticed with a smile.

The banging was really starting to piss him off. He was reminded of
how much he loved the security in his penthouse. No one got through
to his front door. Not without his permission, he thought with a grum-
ble as he pulled his jeans on. He didn't bother snapping the top though,
fully intending to get rid of whoever was pounding, then drag Maggie
back to bed and make love to her all over again.

With that in mind, he came out of the bedroom and looked around.
The sofa still looked sad, but there was an interesting zebra striped print
fabric hanging over the back. Even from across the room, he could
tell that the fabric was thick. Upholstery fabric? He certainly hoped
that Maggie wasn't going to cover that tacky green sofa with the zebra
stripped stuff. That would be pretty hideous.

55

Another bang, followed by, "Maggie!   I know that you're in there! You can't avoid me forever!" Then more banging.

Oliver found Maggie in the kitchen, wearing only the tee shirt he'd discarded last night. It came down to the middle of her thighs and she was still barefoot, dancing with a spatula in one hand as she listened to music with her ear buds. Every few moments, she let out a squeak, as if she were singing along. But she was completely oblivious to the knocking.

With a chuckle, he walked over to the door to her apartment and pulled it open, fully intending to disperse whoever was rudely banging at such an early hour.

But before Oliver could say a word, the idiot stormed into the apartment. "Who are you?" the guy demanded.

Oliver looked him over, noting his expensive suit and four hundred dollar haircut. The guy was slick, Oliver thought. But still a pansy. A bully. Several inches shorter than Oliver and without any muscle tone to fill out the suit, the guy clearly thought he was someone to be reckoned with.

Before Oliver could tell the ass to go away, the man lifted his hand in the air, palm out, stopping the words. "Forget it. I don't care. Where's Maggie? My business is with her. So you need to leave."

Oliver's eyebrows shot up to his hairline, stunned at being dismissed so completely. It had never happened before, so it took a moment for him to fully grasp the stupidity of this man's tone and meaning.

"Excuse me?" Oliver stated as calmly as possible.

The man didn't even bother to repeat his order. He started towards Maggie, who was still in the kitchen, dancing and singing. Well, sort of singing. And still entirely unaware of the scuffle behind her.

Oliver wasn't having it. He might be wearing only a pair of jeans, but he didn't care. Maggie, on the other hand, was only in his tee shirt.

Stepping in the man's path, he glared him down.

The other man's eyes narrowed, as if he were trying to intimidate Oliver somehow. "Buddy, you don't know who you're dealing with!" the shorter man said, dropping his voice as if that would make his presence more threatening.

Oliver snorted. "Sure. Quite the tough guy, aren't you? But you're going to have to wait until Maggie is dressed." And with that, Oliver took the guy by the back of his shirt and, because he was pissed off, shoved him out of the apartment.

"What the hell do you think you're doing?!" the guy bellowed.

"When you can behave like a gentleman, *then* you may speak to Maggie." Oliver leaned down, one hand on the door as he got in the sputtering jerk's face. "That's only *if* she wants to speak with *you*."

With that, he slammed the door and turned to look for Maggie, who was...still dancing. Oblivious to the minor altercation happening in her living room. Or what would be a living room, he thought as he looked at all of the boxes piled up around the edge of the plywood floors. Damn, the woman didn't even have carpeting? What the hell?

Oliver tapped on Maggie's shoulder, startling her into yelping as she spun around. "Oh!" she laughed, putting her free hand to her chest as she leaned back against the counter. "Sorry. I was...making breakfast." She blushed and glanced over her shoulder at the simmering pancakes. "I don't even know if you like breakfast. Or if you work out in the mornings. Or if you even like pancakes. I just...well, I guess I meant to–"

"You have company," Oliver said, interrupting her and pulling her closer so that their hips pressed together.

Maggie pulled the second ear bud out, peering around at the empty room. "I do? Where?"

"Yeah." His hands slid underneath her tee shirt. "He was being rude, so I kicked him out. Plus," he leaned in to tease her neck, "I don't like strangers seeing you like this." He slid his hands underneath the satin of her panties so that he could cup her bare bottom, squeezing to emphasize his point.

The banging started up again and Oliver glared daggers at the door. Looking down at her, he pulled his hands away as he suggested, "Why don't you go get dressed and I'll explain to that idiot that he needs to remember how to act like a gentleman."

Maggie tilted her head. "Who's out there?"

He shrugged. "Some ass who wants to talk to you." He patted her bottom again. "Go get dressed, Maggie. I need to have a few words with the guy."

Maggie smiled, feeling oddly protected. She hadn't had anyone look out for her since her grandmother's funeral. And boy, what a miserable day that had been!

Walking into her bedroom, she quickly pulled on a pair of jeans and, reluctantly giving up the wonderful scent of Oliver's tee-shirt, she snapped a bra on, then one of her own tee-shirts.

Oliver stepped out of the apartment, pulling the door firmly closed behind him and, when the shorter man attempted to push past him again, Oliver rudely shoved him back, making him stumble.

"That's assault!" the man spat, his hands still out in the air as if he needed assistance balancing himself. "I'll have you arrested!"

Oliver crossed his arms over his still-bare chest and frowned down his nose at the man. "Assault?" he scoffed. "Prove it!"

The guy snickered as he straightened up, jerking his jacket back into place. "You really don't know who I am," he said in a softer tone. Oliver suspected that the guy thought that the tone was more threatening, but in reality, he sounded foolish. Oliver knew that he could take him down with a single punch.

But because this guy needed to speak with Maggie, he refrained from breaking his nose.

"You're going to lower your voice and be more respectful," Oliver explained, his own voice becoming more gravelly and *that* was threatening. "When you speak with Maggie, you will treat her with respect and dignity. And you will conduct your business with Maggie in a calmer tone of voice, without disturbing the other residents in this building."

Oliver had no idea if this guy was Maggie's boss or someone else important to her. If the putz was Maggie's boss, then Oliver would protect her. Hell, he could give her a job at any one of his properties at a higher salary. If the shorter man wasn't her boss, Oliver still wasn't threatened. He'd protect Maggie no matter who the jerk was, or what he threatened.

The shorter man's features smoothed out, becoming more assessing. "So, you're the boy toy?" the putz asked, looking smug. It took all of Oliver's control to not wipe that revolting smirk clean off his face.

"I'm Oliver," he replied, extending his hand politely.

The guy took Oliver's hand, tightening his grip more than necessary. Oh, he wanted to play that game? Oliver jerked him closer and squeezed. The putz blinked in surprise and finally started to understand he was in danger.

But the shorter man rallied quickly, puffing up his chest like all bullies tried to do. "I'm Jerry Trevino," the guy sneered, glaring up at Oliver. "And you're going to regret what you've done this morning. I'll make sure that you're fired from whatever pathetic job you have and that you're kicked out of the cave you came from."

Oliver chuckled. "Think you're that powerful?" he asked.

Jerry jerked his hand away, stepped back, then nodded, adjusting his jacket again. "Yeah. I am."

Oliver shrugged dismissively. "Okay, Jerry Trevino. I consider myself adequately warned."

"I'll start by having your ass arrested," the putz threatened.

"For what?" Oliver asked, once again crossing his arms, his feet braced wide as he shrugged casually.

"For assault, you idiot! You pushed me!"

Oliver laughed, shaking his head. "Prove it."

The guy looked around, and found Louise and Nora standing on the sidewalk, watching the altercation with wide, curious eyes. Obviously the elderly ladies had been roused by the noise because they were still in their nightclothes, slippers and robes covering their old-fashioned nightgowns. "I have witnesses."

Louise shook her head. "Honey, all I saw was *you* making a ruckus outside of Maggie's apartment. I didn't see anyone push anything."

Nora nodded in emphatic agreement. "I definitely didn't see Oliver push some weak, pathetic excuse for a maggot away from Maggie's door." She turned to Louise. "Should we call the police and report this guy for disturbing the peace?"

Jerry's jaw went slack. But he pulled himself together. "Right. If that's how you want to play this. Fine." He shook himself and tried again. "I need to speak with Maggie. She and I have business to discuss. So, get the hell out of my way."

The door to Maggie's apartment opened. Maggie stepped around Oliver and frowned. "What's going...?" she stopped when she spotted the putz. "Jerry?"

Oliver's gaze swung from the putz to Maggie, stunned at the change in her tone. "You know him?"

"She's my damn fiancée!" Jerry snapped. "Now get the hell out of my way before I have you arrested!"

Oliver stepped back, too shocked to retort. Then his anger built as he watched that short, annoying man walk over and kiss Maggie. Well, he went for her lips, but Maggie turned away at the last moment so he just caught her cheek. But he managed to wrap his arms around her before she could move out of reach.

He could barely think straight as he watched the man, that insufferably smug expression back on his doughboy face.

"Maggie, do you want me to get rid of this...person?" Oliver asked, praying she'd give the right answer. He needed her to say that she wanted "Jerry" gone, out of her life, and off of this property.

Instead, he watched as she rallied, straightened her shoulders and... shook her head. "No. Thank you, but I'll be fine. I'll speak to him."

Oliver worried he might crack a tooth, clenching his teeth in frustration. After last night...hell, after the past several weeks...Maggie was seriously going to push him away in favor of this putz?

Granted, the putz was her *fiancé*! What the hell was going on here?! Less than an hour ago, she'd been in *his* arms!

He watched as Maggie flinched away from Jerry's touch, but she didn't tell him to leave. "Fine. I just need my shoes," he snapped and pushed past her to go back into her bedroom. Oliver didn't look around as he grabbed his shirt and shoes, not bothering to put them on before turning to walk right back out.

Without hesitating, or even looking back at her, he brushed past her back out the door and walked the two doors down to his own place.

Maggie watched Oliver walk away and wanted to call out to him. She wanted to run over to him and tell him that...what? That she loved him? That was crazy! She'd known Oliver for barely three weeks! There's no way her feelings for him could be that strong. Good grief, she'd known Jerry pretty much all her life and it had taken him over a year of dating before she'd felt comfortable around him. And then she'd been with him for another year before he'd convinced her that she loved him. After which, he'd proposed.

So no, there was no way that she was in love with Oliver.

Still, she should have listened to her instincts about Jerry during those two years before he'd proposed. She'd known, deep down, that they weren't right for each other. But Jerry was pretty insistent. Besides, Jerry had flattered her. He'd teased her and told her that she was the best thing in his life.

He'd convinced her that he needed her.

The slime ball!

As those painful memories came flooding back, she turned and glared at the man. "What do you want?" she demanded flatly.

"Let's not have this reunion in public, my dear," he said softly, but there was a hard glint in his eyes that warned her that Jerry was up to no good.

She pulled back when he reached for her arm. "I think I'm fine right here," she said. "In fact, let's go sit over there," she pointed towards the benches around the fire pit. "I think that it's safer if we have our conversation in public."

He laughed, but it wasn't an amused sound. "Need your pit bull close by?"

She swung around, fury in her eyes. "Don't call him that!" she snapped. "In fact, don't you even speak about Oliver! You're not worthy of even speaking his name!"

Jerry pulled back, lifting his hands up, palms out. "Right! Damn, woman!" Then his lips curled up into a smarmy grin. "You should know better than to give me a weapon like that." He snickered and Maggie narrowed her eyes as he sat down next to her. When he did that, she stood up and moved to a different seat.

"Don't you dare try to hurt Oliver," she whispered with hatred in her voice. "You're slime, Jerry."

He laughed and leaned back, pretending to be unconcerned. "Yeah, I know you think that. But you also know how much power I have. If you cross me, I'll get him fired."

Maggie went still, remembering that first day she'd seen Oliver. He'd been...hung over? She wasn't sure, but Oliver had appeared pretty bedraggled. He was better now. He was wearing new clothes...well, newer clothes and shaved most mornings. He had transportation, even though Mick had mentioned needing to fix something on it. Oliver was finally getting his life back together. He was pulling himself out of the hole that he'd gone into prior to moving here to Rose Gardens.

"You leave him alone!" she snarled, pointing a finger in his direction. "This is between you and me!"

Jerry laughed, more relaxed now that he had the power. "Ah, little Maggie! You've changed. You used to be such a snobby pain in the ass. What happened to you?"

Maggie pressed her lips together and didn't respond.

"Found Jesus or something?" he mocked. "Whatever," he waved his question away and leaned forward, bracing his elbows on his knees. "Thing is, I want your land."

"No."

"You're going to sell it to me," he continued, ignoring her reaction.

"Why do you think I'd do anything to help you?"

"Because I want your land. I'm willing to pay for it." He looked pointedly around, still sneering. "You obviously need the money." He locked eyes with her. "And if you don't sell me the damn land, I'll get your pretty boy toy fired."

He stood up and pulled a card out of his pocket, and threw it at her. "And because you're being such a stubborn little bitch, I'm cutting my offer in half. Call me when you start thinking with your brain instead of your..." his eyes dropped to her groin area, then snickered. "Well, whatever it is that women have that is the mediocre equivalent of a dick."

Jerry laughed heartily as he walked away.

Maggie stared after him, wondering why he'd come all this way just to threaten her. Goodness, she hated that man! She hated Jerry and everything he stood for. She hated him for how he'd hurt her, how he'd degraded her, humiliated her, and she hated him now because he dared threaten someone she lo...cared very deeply for.

Glancing over at Oliver's door, she stood up, wiped the despised tears from her cheeks and walked back into her apartment.

Staring at the mess, she sobbed once before she caught herself. Gulping back the anger and emotions that she refused to let loose, she took the stack of pancakes that she'd so happily cooked this morning and tossed everything into the trash. She wasn't hungry and she'd only made a double batch because she knew how much Oliver could eat. He had a metabolism that never seemed to stop.

It was all trash now, she told herself. Plus, her perfect little world, her oasis from the reality of her past life, all that shame had broken through the protective walls she'd built up around herself. Jerry's visit had tarnished her world, made her feel filthy all over again.

Oliver stomped around his apartment, packing up everything that he'd brought from his penthouse. No way was he sticking around now. Maggie was engaged? That's twice that he'd trusted a woman and been lied to. Damn it, when was he going to learn? Why was he such a sap when it came to women?

No more! He was done! Finished! He'd get the hell out of here and get back to his real life. A place where the damned light switches worked and there was unlimited hot water! And where the cabinet doors weren't falling off the hinges! Damn he couldn't wait to get the hell out of this apartment.

A knock on his door drew his attention and snapped him out of his contemplation of a long swim in his heated pool. All by his damn self! No neighbors sneaking over to 'check in' on him. No girls asking if he'd show them a few more soccer tricks. No...no one to deliver cookies when they thought he was having a rough day.

Another knock, this time more urgent, pulled at his attention. He opened his eyes, unaware of having closed them. He glare at the offending door and, with a growl because he assumed it was the putz coming back for another round, he opened his mouth to threaten the little bastard if he didn't get the hell away from the door.

"Maggie needs help," Eddie announced through the door, wringing his aging hands together. He glanced at Maggie's door, then back to Oliver, who opened his door.

"She'll be fine," Oliver sighed. "She's tough. She can handle anything." Which was the truth, he thought.

Eddie shook his head. "Not that guy, she can't. And he didn't really threaten her so much as you."

It took a moment for the Eddie's words to sink in. Threaten? Who was threatening Maggie? No, not Maggie. The putz was threatening *him*? That was new! "Me? How did that ass threaten me? If he calls the police, he'll just–"

"No! It has nothing to do with that shoving match earlier, the one

which no one saw any way," Eddie said quickly and with a pointed look
that warned Oliver that the whole apartment complex stood behind
him. "The guy that came by this morning and woke all of us up, he
threatened you, Oliver. He told Maggie that he'd get you fired from
your job if she didn't sell him something."

That wasn't what he'd anticipated. And it didn't make any sense,
either. What could the man have over Maggie? What did Jerry want
from her that he wouldn't get as soon as they were married?

Maggie's door was still closed. "Is he still here?"

Eddie shook his head. "Maggie wouldn't let him inside her apartment.
I heard her say that it was safer if she and the stranger talked out in
public. She brought him over to the fire pit."

She didn't feel safe with her fiancé? "Why would she...?"

But Eddie wasn't finished. "And when he sat down too close to her,
Maggie jumped up as if he'd stabbed her and changed seats."

Oliver stared at the elderly man, stumped. Maggie had moved away
from Jerry? That didn't sound like something she'd do with a man
she'd promised to marry. And she didn't feel safe alone with Jerry
in her apartment? Maggie was willing to risk everyone in the entire
apartment complex hearing their conversation? And Maggie had to
know that they'd be listening. These people loved to know each others'
business.

"He's trouble, Oliver! You have to fix this! Maggie is terrified and I'm
afraid she's going to do something stupid to try to protect you!"

Oliver's head snapped up, as if Eddie had slapped him. His eyes
swung over to Maggie's door. This didn't make sense! And there was
only one way to find out what was going on.

"Thanks, Eddie," he said patting his shoulder. "I'll take care of it."

Eddie visibly relaxed and Oliver stepped out of his apartment. He
had shoes on now and walked down the sidewalk towards Maggie's
apartment. Knocking softly on the door, he waited. But Maggie didn't
answer.

"Maggie, open up. We need to talk."

Maggie appeared in the doorway and sniffed. He could tell that she'd
been crying although she tried to hide it. She'd wiped her tears away,
but her eyes were red from the tears. Plus, the smile she bestowed
upon him didn't light up her eyes. Nope, something was seriously
wrong.

"What's up?" she asked. "I'm sorry if you're hungry. I ate all the
pancakes."

Oliver pushed the door wider and stepped into her apartment. "Is he
gone?" he demanded, closing the door when Jerry didn't appear. Damn

it, he was going to get someone in here to carpet her place. The idea of Maggie getting a splinter from this particleboard flooring.... And he was angry enough now to make it an issue.

"Yes. Jerry left," she replied, crossing her arms protectively over her stomach and backing away.

Oliver paced through the kitchen, reeling with questions. But when he looked down, he noticed the full trashcan. "You threw out your pancakes? You just told me you ate them."

Maggie shrugged, rubbing her forehead. "Well, I...Oliver, you need to go." She stared down at her bare toes. "Just...I don't...it isn't a good idea for you to be here."

He watched her carefully and something clicked into his mind. But he needed more information before he could make a plan. "I think you owe me an explanation, Maggie."

She turned away and he saw her blinking back more tears. "We're engaged. What's more to say?"

He felt the slash of pain at the thought of that putz touching Maggie. But...no, something didn't feel right. He kept watching. Open, honest, and wonderful Maggie....no, she wasn't engaged. Maggie would never flirt with him, much less share her body with him and make love with him so completely like she'd done last night if she were engaged. It just wasn't the way she was made.

"You're not engaged."

Her shoulders stiffened and, instantly, he knew that he was right. "I... was."

Okay, he could see that. Well, maybe not. Maggie was just too sweet and kind and generous. A guy like that would have crushed her spirit. This was not a crushed woman. "What happened? Why aren't you still engaged to him?"

She pulled her arms tighter across her body. "I...uh...discovered that I wasn't in love with him."

He waited. Because he knew that there was more. "And?"

Maggie stared out the window, but he doubted that her eyes took in the beauty of the courtyard.

"Two years ago, my grandmother died," she began. "My mother died right after giving birth to me and my father vanished at the same time. It was just my grandmother and me." Maggie sighed. "My grandmother was one of those amazing women who grew up under the hot, Texas sunshine and only got tougher with age. She took over her father's cattle ranch and built it into something..." she sighed. "Incredible."

"She sounds like a wonderful woman."

Maggie looked up, blinking quickly in an attempt to manage her tears. "She was. My grandmother spoiled me rotten. Anything I wanted, she'd give me. One of the ranch hands built me a princess bed and a castle in my bedroom for my fifth birthday. When I turned twelve, I wanted a pool, so my grandmother installed one in the backyard. When I turned sixteen, I got a car." She laughed. "I didn't have a driver's license because I'd failed the test. But I wanted one, so she gave it to me."

"You were spoiled?" he repeated, startled.

Maggie peeked at Oliver through her eyelashes. "I was an absolute brat," she confirmed.

"What happened?"

Maggie wished that this had never come up. But now that Jerry had shown up, now that Oliver's job and success were in danger, Maggie knew that he deserved the truth.

"Then, my grandmother died."

"And you inherited everything?"

Maggie nodded. "Every last debt."

Oliver cringed as he grasped the meaning of her words. "She was out of money."

"And hiding it from me." Maggie paced around the small space. "My grandmother was a proud woman. She didn't want anyone to know how badly her financial status had changed. But on the day she died, I took over everything. Her lawyer told me that she had no cash on hand, the house was heavily mortgaged, and she was in debt up to her eyeballs." Maggie took another deep breath. "That was also the day that Jerry found out about my grandmother's lack of wealth. He immediately broke off our engagement and demanded I return the three carat diamond ring."

She laughed softly and slumped down onto the sofa. "I had to grow up fast. I also realized that all of the people I thought were my friends, actually hated me. With a vengeance."

"I doubt that."

She shook her head sadly. "No, they *really* did. And I can't even blame them. I had to take a good hard look at my grandmother's finances. I realized a lot of the debts came from keeping me happy. I grew up a lot that day. It was difficult, but I took on the responsibility of selling off anything that I could in order to pay my grandmother's debts. All of the cattle were sold first. The entire ranch staff were let go, which only caused more animosity from the townspeople, because my grandmother employed several dozen people. It took me over a year to sell the house because there really aren't that many people that could afford a house that big. I sold my car, my grandmother's jewelry, all of the furniture, and anything else that wasn't bolted down." She sighed. "I managed to raise enough to pay off every debt. But I was broke. Broke, homeless, and hated by everyone I knew."

"And then you came here?"

She nodded. "Yep. I needed a fresh start." She turned and looked at him. "I needed to prove to myself that I wasn't a bad person." She looked down at her hands, noticed the scrapes and bruises. Years ago, she would have been horrified by the way her hands and nails looked. But now, she felt every scrape and bruise, every scar and cracked nail, was a badge of honor. She put in an honest day's work and she'd turned these buildings around. And even ran the place at a profit!

"I'm good at my job, Oliver," she told him, defensively. "I'm good at my job and I'm trying so hard to be a good person."

He pulled her onto his lap. "I think you're a beautiful and incredibly wonderful person, Maggie."

She sniffed and blinked back a fresh wave of tears. "But you thought I'd have sex with you when I was engaged to someone else."

He pressed a kiss to the top of her head. "Only because you didn't deny the guy's claim on you."

She shivered and he tightened his arms around her. "I was in shock. He said we were engaged and, well, I didn't immediately deny it because I never expected to see him here, on my doorstep. I felt as if his presence here would rightfully ruin the happiness that I'd found. I'd hurt so many people in my life, and maybe I don't deserve to feel this way. Maybe I'm still the selfish, horrible person I was then."

"I don't think you're selfish or horrible. You've built a good life for yourself here. You're good, kind, and very generous."

She sniffed, shaking her head. "I'm not. And even if others think I am now, I have so much more to make up for. My past still haunts me, Oliver."

He pulled her closer and Maggie leaned into him, absorbing his goodness and strength.

"You're a good person, Maggie. You're doing amazing things here. Everyone loves you. I think you should stop beating yourself up for your past and start accepting that you've changed."

"It's not enough. If it was, then Jerry wouldn't be here, messing things up."

There was silence after that and Maggie took his silence for his agreement. She tried to slip off of his lap, not allowing herself the comfort of his embrace. But he wouldn't let her go. Instead, he tightened his arms around her.

"What does Jerry have over you?" he asked softly.

She froze, confused. "What do you mean?"

"Eddie came to me and told me that he threatened you. He said that if you didn't do something, then he would get me fired." He pulled away and looked at her. "What was Jerry threatening you with?"

Maggie stared at him for a long moment, then laughed, shaking her head. "It's nothing that I've done," she promised. "It's actually something I *won't* do." She slipped off his lap and stepped away, again wrapping her arms around her waist. "I sold off everything of value I inherited in Texas in order to pay off the debts from my grandmother's estate. But there was one thing that I couldn't sell. It's a strip of land along a river. At the time, it wasn't valuable. In fact, I was pretty frustrated that I couldn't snip that last tie to Texas and move on with my life. I've been paying the property taxes on that stupid piece of land for a while." She sighed, rubbing her forehead. "Actually, it's not a stupid piece of land. It's beautiful. It's a large strip of land out in an area that some might call the middle of nowhere, but there are hundreds of big, graceful trees and a beautiful river meanders through. Lots of animals come for water there and it's pretty idyllic in a quiet, peaceful kind of way."

"And Jerry wants you to sell him that piece of land?" he asked.

Maggie laughed bitterly. "Yes. Apparently, he's bought up all of the land around mine and wants to develop it."

"I thought it was in the middle of nowhere? What's the point of developing land and building on it if the land isn't close to anything?"

She smiled, leaning her head back and closing her eyes. "I've heard through the grapevine that someone came through several months ago and worked with the state. They agreed to pay for the roads leading into the area if the land could be rezoned for residential and retail use. Jerry heard about the offer from the state, which would incorporate my former small town to the Dallas county limits." She smiled ruefully at Oliver. "Another little tidbit that I discovered was that the town doesn't want the development. They don't want the land to be turned into yet another suburban sprawl with all of the golf courses and strip malls that are so bad for the environment." She sighed heavily. "So, not selling to Jerry is my way of paying the town back for all of the horrible things that I put them through when I was a kid."

Oliver looked around at her apartment, again noting the lack of furniture except for the pieces she was trying to refinish herself. Suddenly, it came together. The puzzle pieces connected in his mind and he felt something pop deep down inside himself. Standing up, he asked, "You're using all your salary to pay the taxes on that land, aren't you?"

Maggie shrugged and nodded slowly. "Yeah. I am. And Jerry has put the screws in by convincing the county financial office to increase the taxes on that piece of land. He's trying to make it so that the land is too expensive for me to keep." She sighed, pulling her lips into a cringe. "He's actually closer to winning than he knows."

Oliver pulled her back into his arms. For a long moment, they just stood there. Maggie closed her eyes and wished that this morning had gone differently.

"He's threatening to make my life miserable if you don't sell him the land." It was a statement, not a question. Oliver understood what was going on. He never played that way when working his development deals. But he knew that his competitors played dirty when necessary. Oliver preferred to go a more ethical route by only developing in areas where the landowners were willing to sell.

However, he'd rarely considered the neighborhoods in which he'd planned to develop. And his thoughts came back to what he was doing to this neighborhood. His team had approached each of the land and building owners in the area with offers to buy their property. Every one of them had been eager to sell. But what about the residents in the neighborhoods? What about the Community Center down the street? And the smaller homes along the residential streets? Yes, their property values would increase. But for these people, that only meant that their property taxes would increase. Many of them wouldn't be able to afford it and would be forced to sell out and move.

What would that mean for their lives? How would it impact their friendships? Their kids? The schools? The spirit of community that had built up over the years? This entire community had worked together to make this area their own oasis.

That wasn't something that Oliver had considered over the years.

But now that he knew what might happen, he was going to fix it. He wasn't sure how, but he'd figure something out.

"Don't sell out to Jerry the Putz," he urged.

"I might have to," she whispered back, hiding her face against his chest. Oliver could tell she was crying again. For him! Damn, that felt really good! Little Maggie, fierce and fearless Maggie, was going to sacrifice something important to her because...hell, because he was more important to her!

Aw hell! Damn, he...loved her! Really loved her! He'd been fighting that knowledge for too long, but now that he'd accepted it, a feeling of rightness washed over him. Peace? Yes. There was a feeling of peaceful rightness.

"You don't have to sell. Let me make some calls."

She pulled back and looked up at him. "But what about...?"

He kissed her. It was a soft kiss of promise and it silenced her worries. When he lifted his head again, he smiled down at her. "My job is secure, Maggie. Don't you dare sell out to Jerry the Putz just to protect me. I guarantee that he can't affect my job in any way."

"But–"

His eyes hardened at her continued skepticism. "Maggie, I need you to trust me, okay?"

Oliver watched as she processed his words. He saw the moment she understood and he felt relief surge through him. He suspected that Jerry could become pretty desperate. Oliver knew that he'd have to get his team to look into the situation in Texas. It shouldn't be too difficult to get information. Once he had the facts, he'd ensure that Jerry's threats were neutralized. Even more, he planned to do a bit more than simply neutralize the man's mischief. After all, Jerry the Putz had threatened Oliver's woman.

Oliver was going to crush the bastard!

Chapter 11

"Get Burt in my office immediately," Oliver ordered his assistant as soon as he stepped out of the elevator.

Jamie nodded and grabbed his phone, making the call while Oliver walked into his office, tossing some papers onto his desk. He sat down and started clicking through tax information, his lips compressing as he mentally calculated how much Maggie was paying in personal property taxes on that damn piece of land. He looked at it carefully, then clicked on other links to find the tax assessments for the other pieces of land.

By the time Burt, the head of his legal department, entered the office, Oliver was furious.

"What's up, Oliver?" Burt asked, his easy stride demonstrating the man's confidence.

Oliver leaned back in his leather chair.

"There's a small town in Texas that is pressuring a woman to sell her property by increasing her taxes by astronomical amounts."

Burt took the paper Oliver handed him, skimming the numbers. The man gave a whistle of surprise at the data, shaking his head. "Well, this is an interesting little problem," he said, taking out his pen and writing something on the paper. "Is this one of your projects?"

"No. We're not involved in this land or tax issue in any way."

Burt cocked an eyebrow. "So, if we have no horse in this race, why do we care about this? I mean, yeah, it's unconstitutional to levy taxes for the sole purpose of pushing someone out of ownership, which," he looked from the paper to Oliver, "I'm assuming this is what this outrageous tax assessment is all about?"

"That's my suspicion," Oliver replied.

Burt nodded. "Okay, so if this isn't...?"

"It's definitely for the benefit of this company," he replied, interrupting

Burt. "This is a dear friend who is being punished because she won't sell to some guy for development purposes. I want you to go down to Texas and sue the county for back taxes, plus interest, as well as punitive damages."

Burt laughed, startled by this unprecedented command. "Why?"

"It's personal," was all Oliver said.

Burt frowned at the numbers again. "If this information is correct, it should be relatively easy to come to a settlement. Most small counties rely on no one protesting their tax assessments because they don't have the financial or legal resources."

"I agree. Which is why I want punitive damages. This county had been taxing the owner of this land and hoping that she doesn't have the resources to fight them. She's simply been paying the taxes to the detriment of her health."

Burt tensed. "Do you have proof of that?"

"Yeah. I can get you pictures of her current residence. She doesn't even have carpeting, just plywood. No furniture. I can get you bank statements too, if needed, to show that she's been spending the majority of her income on the increased taxes."

Burt contemplated that for a moment, then nodded. "Okay. I bet I can make a pretty good argument. I'll get back to you on the documents I'll need."

"Good," Oliver said. "There's something else." He pressed on his intercom button. "Jamie, can you get Tom from security in here?"

Burt's eyes widened, but while they waited for Tom, the two men chatted about an upcoming golf tournament, which Oliver commented that he wouldn't be attending, not bothering to mention he needed to help coach a girls' soccer game.

A few minutes into their conversation, Tom, the head of his security department, entered the office.

"What's up, boss?" Tom asked, nodding to Burt.

Oliver leaned back in his chair as the two men took a seat. "Tom, I want you to dig up whatever you can on a guy named Jerry Trevino. Burt is going down to Texas to file suit against a small town that has been imposing punitive tax assessments against the owner of a piece of land down there. But I need you to look into this Trevino guy, who I know is involved. Find out what he's up to. Get his financial information and whatever businesses he's got. He's trying to develop a swath of land down in Texas and something doesn't smell right. We have several projects in that area and I want to make sure that there isn't something bigger going on."

For the next fifteen minutes, the three men discussed what Oliver knew of the land development project that Trevino was working on and a few other topics.

When the men left Oliver's office, he leaned back in his chair and contemplated his next move. He had to be patient though. He needed the information from Tom before he could formulate a plan that would destroy the weasel who had dared threaten Maggie.

Chapter 12

A week later, Oliver stepped out of his truck and Maggie almost threw herself into his arms. "Are you okay?" Maggie demanded. She'd been waiting for him all day.

"I'm fine," he replied, his wonderfully strong arms wrapping around her and pulling her in close. "Why are you so worried?"

She pulled out of his arms and glared up at him, punching him lightly on the arm. "Because you weren't here with me when I woke up this morning," she explained angrily. "And you didn't answer my messages!"

He sighed and pulled her back into his arms. "I'm sorry, honey." He kissed her lightly. "I was in meetings all day. But I should have texted you. I'm sorry. I will do better."

Slightly mollified, she shrugged. "I was just...worried that maybe Jerry was still in town."

"He isn't. He flew back to Texas late last night."

Maggie blinked, confused, but he put his arm around her waist and led her away from the parking lot. "How in the world could you know that?"

He chuckled and kissed the top of her head. "Oh, I have a few resources that I can pull in when I need information," he said vaguely. "But we're not going to worry about Jerry the Putz tonight."

"We're not?" she laughed, thinking he was so darn sexy.

"Nope. I need your help with something."

She laughed again, playfully slipping out of his arms but he grabbed her easily, pulling her right back to his side. "Oh no!" she teased. "You said something yesterday about helping me in my shower. And then we ran out of hot water while I still had shampoo in my hair."

He shot her an evil grin. "I didn't hear you complaining before the hot water ran out," he growled, nipping at her earlobe.

Maggie shivered. "That's because you were...well...doing *that* and...!" she stopped speaking but the hot blush washed over her face.

"Yeah. I remember. You weren't complaining," he came right back. "In fact, I distinctly remember you saying something along the lines of 'don't stop' and 'oh yes' as well as many other very emphatic phrases." He shook his head in mock despair. "You know that I'm a gentleman and would have stopped if I'd known you were worried about running out of hot water."

She groaned. "You're horrible." She also hugged his arm. "What do you need help with?"

He kissed her again and she smiled, leaning her head against his muscular shoulder as they walked down the sidewalk towards their apartments.

"Come with me," he said, and led her to his apartment. After unlocking the door, he pulled her inside and...Maggie gasped.

"What have you done?" she demanded, stepping into the apartment and turning slowly around. "This...this isn't the apartment that I gave you over a month ago, Oliver."

He grinned, leaning back against the door. "What do you think?"

She stopped, admiring the dove grey walls with the freshly painted white trim...all of which had been replaced. The outlets had been fixed, with new equipment, and the popcorn ceiling had been smoothed over and repainted. Even the overhead lights had been upgraded. The eighties style dome lights had been replaced with recessed lighting! It looked amazing!

"When did you have time to do all of this, Oliver?" she asked softly. But she came to a stop when her eyes took in the kitchen area. "The cabinets...?" she whispered.

"I took them down."

"But..." her eyes moved lower. "You painted the old cabinets?"

"Yes. And fixed the hardware. The cabinet doors close properly now."

She nodded dumbly, then lifted her hand, pointing towards the beautiful, ornate tile backsplash. "The tiles?" she whispered.

He turned and looked over at the kitchen wall. "Yeah," he muttered, rubbing a hand along the back of his neck. "That was before that morning in the laundry room," he explained with a chuckle. "I was pretty frustrated."

She turned, unaware of her mouth hanging open as she looked up at him. "Frustrated?"

He nodded, walking over to her. He stopped right in front of her, putting his hands on her hips and pulling her closer. "Yeah. You kept walking around in those tight jeans and–"

"My jeans aren't that tight!" she corrected, her hands flying to her butt as if her hands could hide the body part in question.

He chuckled. "Tight enough for me to drool every time I watched you running across the courtyard. Away from me."

Maggie shuffled uncomfortably. "I wasn't running away from you."

His hands slid along her waist, teasing her by not touching her breasts.

"Yeah, you were," he countered. "You were running and I wasn't chasing for fear of driving you further away. It wasn't until I showed up at the girls' soccer practice that I finally got a chance to have a conversation with you."

Maggie looked flustered and he loved it! "Well, that was…just…I wasn't…!"

"It's all good now," he told her and kissed her gently. "After meeting Jerry the Putz, I understand why you were running. You didn't want to be hurt again."

She stared up at him, startled that he understood so completely. "Yes. Well. He asked for my engagement ring back at my grandmother's funeral."

Oliver emitted a sound of disgust, shaking his head. "He's an ass, Maggie," Oliver declared. "That was unnecessarily cruel."

Maggie slipped her arms up around his neck, so she could run her fingers through his hair. "So…what kind of help did you need?" she asked. "It looks as if you've done more than fine so far."

He shifted his hips and, after a smile that should have warned her of his intent, he lifted her up and placed her on the wood countertop behind her.

"What are you doing?" she half-laughed, half-shrieked, trying to wiggle off the counter.

"I need you right here," he said as his hands slid up her sides to cup her breasts, teasing the already taut nipples.

Maggie gasped, arching her back, but when he started to move his hands away, she grabbed his wrists, keeping them in place. "More," she whispered.

In response, Oliver pinched her nipples, inciting a whimper of pleasure and Maggie leaned into his touch, already desperate with need.

"Please, don't stop!"

"Not a chance", he replied. His mouth moved to cover those lusciously abused peaks, adding the moist heat to the pressure of his finger. Tightening his fingers as his tongue lashed the tips, Maggie was completely lost to the sensations. Her fingers dove into his hair, pulling and tugging, then holding him in place when she thought he might stop. She felt his mouth curl into a smile, but Maggie was too far gone to make sense of that smile.

A second later, she was lifted into his arms, roughly carried to...somewhere. She felt something soft against her back, but couldn't think beyond getting his clothes off of him so that she could feel the roughness of his chest against her already sensitive nipples.

"Oliver!" she whispered...or moaned...either adjective might apply at this moment.

"Tell me what you want," he growled, nipping in her ear.

"You!" she replied quickly, shifting her hips against his, telling him without words.

He pulled her tee-shirt up and over her head, tossing it to the side. Maggie didn't like the inequity of that, so she slid her hands from his hair, all the way down his arms...then lower until she could feel the tanned skin of his abdomen. With exquisite pleasure, she pushed the material higher and higher. When he took over the removal, Maggie concentrated on kissing the wide expanse of his chest, her tongue flicking out occasionally to taste. She smiled, loving the sounds that he made whenever she did that.

Slowly, she moved lower, pushing at Oliver's shoulders when he started to take control. "Not this time," she told him, letting her fingers slide over his chest, ensuring that her fingertips grazed over his flat, male nipples. She smiled when a shudder rocked his big body, then pressed him backwards, shifting so that she was on top of him.

"Think you're in control?" he asked, his hands sliding underneath her jeans, his big hands palming her butt.

"Yeah," she whispered, kissing his stomach as her fingers fiddled with the button on his jeans. Slowly, watching his face as her fingers lowered the zipper, making sure that her knuckles brushed against the straining erection, she pushed the denim out of the way. A second later, she was lifted off of him and Maggie opened her mouth to protest. But Oliver merely stood up, shucked off his jeans and boxers, then laid back down on his back, pulling her back into position.

"Nice," she laughed softly, then proceeded to kiss her way lower and lower.

"Maggie, I can't..."

"Let me," she urged, glancing up at him. "Please?"

He made some sort of sound, but Maggie was too turned on to interpret what he was trying to tell her. So instead, she wrapped her fingers around his erection, her tongue flicking against the tip. Oliver might have said something, or perhaps it was just another sound. Maggie wasn't sure as she licked and kissed and explored with her tongue, her fingers and her mouth. When she finally wrapped her mouth around his shaft, Oliver hissed as if she'd just burned him. Maggie ignored those sounds and continued to taste and explore and...well, generally see how far she could push him.

Not very far, it turns out. Oliver's hands lifted her up, pulling her so that she was once again straddling his waist. His hands gripped her hips, then slid up to cup her breasts. "Payback, Maggie," he warned her as his thumbs flicked against her nipples.

A second later, he slid lower. Maggie was so startled by his movement, she looked down. She had barely a brief glance at the mischievous look in his eyes before his hands gripped her hips and his mouth... his mouth! Dear heaven, his mouth latched onto that swollen nub and Maggie almost cried. Losing her balance, she reached out to grip the wall, her hips rolling so that his mouth was hitting the right spot. Vaguely, she felt Oliver's hands on her hips again, holding her in place, but Maggie was lost to conscious thought as Oliver's magical mouth did that thing...and his tongue!

The climax crept up on her this time. It was slow and lazy, Oliver's tongue darting out at exactly the right pace to bring her higher and higher, but not over the edge. Maggie whimpered, her fingers curling into fist. She wanted to hit him! She wanted to...do something! She wasn't sure what!

With a cry of outrage, she tried to move away from him. She was so close! So frustratingly close! But Oliver wasn't...he wasn't doing it right! And that just...!

"Stay here," Oliver ordered.

The tone! Oh, the tone! It was so full of command and power and she wanted to hit him and love him and kiss him and...! "Yes!" she whimpered, reaching down to grab a hunk of his hair. "Yes!" she screamed now as he applied his tongue to that nub, his mouth closing over it and sucking until the climax was rushing through her, causing her whole body to shiver and shake and tumble!

Oliver wanted to roar with satisfaction as he grabbed hold of Maggie, shifting their positions so that he was over her now. He grabbed a condom and, while he rolled the protection down over himself, looked at her smile of amazement. He'd done that to her! He wanted to beat his chest and howl. Instead, he took one of her legs, pulled her knee up over his shoulder, then thrust into her heat. The smile was gone, replaced by a stunned expression. Her eyes widened, but her hips shifted to accommodate him.

"You're mine!" he growled, needing to banish that bastard from Maggie's mind. He never wanted her to think of that prick again. Only him. He wanted to imprint himself on her, both her body and her soul, until she couldn't think of anything or anyone but him! Because god knew that she was about all he could think about lately! It was only fair that she was in the same state of torment that he was in all the time.

Thrusting slowly at first, then picking up speed as she lifted her hips, meeting him thrust for thrust until he felt the sharp prickles of her fingernails against his skin. That's when he knew she was close! So beautifully close! Her eyes had been closed, but when she was this close, her eyes opened and she looked up at him. He understood that look. She wasn't sure what to do. Maggie, his beautiful Maggie, wasn't sure how to bring herself over that edge. And it made Oliver want to howl with righteous perfection as he shifted his hips, his finger sliding down over her stomach to tease that too-sensitive nub until....! Damn, she was so beautiful as she thrust against him as another climax hit her, causing those inner muscles to clench around his shaft so tightly, Oliver couldn't hold back another second. Everything went blank as the pleasure hit him and he poured himself into her body.

When it was all over, Oliver collapsed against her, pulling her into his arms as he tried to bring enough oxygen into his lungs. Maggie! His Maggie! Damn, she was so perfect!

Maggie sighed and opened her eyes, staring at the clean, white ceiling. "Wow!" she sighed.

He laughed and the vibrations tickled her stomach where his mouth rested against the soft curve of her belly. "Is that because of the ceiling that used to be yellow and mysteriously stained? Or was your response due to my superior skills as a lover?"

Maggie bit her lip and pretended to think about his question for a moment, then giggled when he swatted her playfully on her bottom. "Well, the ceiling is *very* impressive!"

With a growl, he scooped her up and carried her off to the bedroom. "You'll pay for that my dear," he warned her. Then set her down on the new bathroom vanity and moved over to turn on the shower.

"Good grief, Oliver!" Maggie breathed, looking around at the sparkling new white tiles and the pristine black and white tile flooring. "How in the world did you get all this done so fast?" she asked.

He explained while he tested the water temperature. "I told you, I was frustrated watching you wiggle that cute butt around in those jeans. I needed an outlet, something to focus on instead of wondering how to get in your panties."

She laughed and wrapped her arms around his shoulders as he picked her up again. "Crude, and yet, somehow flattering."

"You are beautiful," he replied, kissing her lips. "You are sexy, smart, and beyond lovely."

She giggled. "Better." She kissed him as he put her down in the shower. "And you are handsome, sexy, and," she leaned up to press a kiss to his lips, "I love exploring every inch of this magnificent body of yours."

Oliver shook his head as he grabbed the soap. "You're just trying to distract me, woman," he growled and spun her around so that her back was to his chest so that he could soap her up. "But it won't work! I have chores for you. I need your help, if you'll recall."

Maggie cracked up. "I wasn't the one who put me on the counter!" She snatched the soap before he could get too friendly with it and spun around, rubbing the bar of soap over his massive chest and shoulders and biceps and...well, everywhere. "You're the one who started the distractions." Although, Maggie was intensely distracted at the moment.

Chapter 13

Desiree tapped her pen against her notebook impatiently as she watched Oliver walk out of the conference room. But 'walk' was the wrong term. He rushed out of the conference room. He'd been doing that a lot lately and it irritated the hell out of her!

How was she supposed to corner him to convince him to take her back into that huge, lovely penthouse if she couldn't even get two words out before he was through the door? Months ago, the first time she'd gotten to him, she'd simply sauntered into his office after hours. He'd been working so hard and she'd convinced him to take a break and grab a drink with her. After that, it had been easy enough to get him to drive her home, since he was such a damn gentleman. Inviting him into her apartment had been the next step, even though it had taken her about a month of drinks and boring chitchat to get him through the door.

Damn him, what the hell was going on? He didn't work late anymore, so she couldn't sneak into his office after hours. These days, he didn't come in early either. She'd even gotten up at the ungodly hour of five o'clock so she could be at her beautiful best when he walked in at seven, which is when he used to get in to work when she'd lived with him.

But lately, the man had been sauntering in around eight o'clock like a normal person! And that really scared her. Because Oliver wasn't normal. He was brilliant and handsome and...good grief, did he ever know what to do with that body. And hers, she thought with a smile.

So, why was he coming in "late" and leaving "early"?

Desiree stalked out of the conference room, furious with herself for letting this situation get away from her, as well as disgusted that she hadn't fixed it already. That smug, pain in the ass of an assistant didn't even let her sneak into his office during the workday. He guarded Oli-

80

ver's office like a dragon guards its hoard!

Taking a deep breath, she put her hands on her hips and looked out the window. Damn, she loved this town. Washington, D.C. was the powerhouse of the country! She loved rubbing elbows with the rich and powerful. The senators and congress members wanted to court Oliver, get him to build something in their states to increase jobs and employment, which would bring in more tax dollars.

Damn, she missed those lovely parties that Oliver was always invited to. He'd scorned so many of those invitations before she'd met him. But Desiree knew how to whine and wheedle with the best of them. Eventually, she'd convinced Oliver to attend, telling him that it was good for business.

Good for *her* business, she thought with a malicious chuckle.

"Desiree, do you have those reports for the next marketing campaign?" Mark, her boss, asked from the doorway.

She smiled over her shoulder. "Yep. I have them right here," she told him and reached for the file folder she'd prepared yesterday. The campaign was great and she was proud of her work, but boy, she really needed a spa day! This working-every-single-day crap was irritating as hell!

"That's great!" Mark replied, visibly relieved as he took the file and hurried off.

As soon as he was gone, Desiree's smile dropped. She was really starting to hate this job. She wasn't made for the daily grind. She wanted so much more for herself than working a nine to five job!

Of course, she didn't actually work from nine to five. It was more like...well, ten to two. Sometimes less than that. None of her tasks were particularly challenging, so she could get her work done in just a few hours.

Still, what was she going to do about Oliver? She wanted back into his life and his bed!

Deciding that it was time to find out, she collected her purse and marched out the door. She didn't care if Mark saw her leave. She was on a mission to get her man and her credit cards back!

Chapter 14

"Get in front of it!" Maggie called out, racing along the white line of the soccer field. "You can do it, Angela!"

The twelve year old Angela glanced around, controlling the ball exactly how Oliver had taught her, dribbling down the soccer field, pulling away from her opponent when she tried to steal the ball. Total control, Maggie thought, almost bursting with pride.

"Behind you!" Oliver yelled.

Maggie didn't bother to look over her shoulder, she knew he was there. Somehow, she always knew where Oliver was. It was as if her mind and her body was aware of him at all times.

"You're open! Go for it!" Maggie urged.

Wendy raced up alongside Angela, guarding her and blocking the opponent. Angela used Wendy's protection to sprint forward. She feinted right, and the goalie shifted right as well. Maggie knew exactly what Angela was going to do even as she did it. She moved further to the right, stopped, then kicked the ball to the far left where Mindy had raced up the field. Mindy took the ball and shot it right into the net! The goalie didn't stand a chance; she was still protecting the right side of the goal. Seconds later, the referee blasted her whistle three times, indicating the end of the game.

Maggie threw her hands in the air and jumped around, clapping until her hands hurt!

"We won!" she yelled. Immediately, victorious twelve and thirteen year old girls surrounded Maggie and Oliver. They'd just beaten the best team in the league and had won the season! They'd actually won! The score was three to two and they'd won!

Oliver high fived each ecstatic player. After a few minutes of celebration, Maggie clapped her hands and pointed towards the center of the field. "Be good sports," she reminded her team.

The girls, still grinning from ear to ear, lined up and walked to the center of the field, hand slapping the other team and congratulating them on a good game. Maggie and Oliver followed behind and even went to the other team coaches, telling them what a great team they had. After thanking the referees, the girls returned to the sidelines, still euphoric as they gathered up their bags, stuffed their reusable water bottles back into their packs, and collected the soccer balls. Meanwhile, Oliver had gone to his truck and lugged a huge cooler back towards the team, but out of the way of the next two teams who were getting ready to play.

"Congratulations, ladies," he said, putting the cooler down and opening it with a flourish to reveal ice cream bars. He handed out ice cream to each player, as well as their siblings that had come to watch the game. There were even enough left over for all of the parents to have one.

Maggie stood back from the crowd, beaming at Oliver's generosity. She had no idea how much money he earned each week, but those ice cream bars had made the girls smile. He was so incredibly thoughtful!

She turned away, afraid that Oliver might notice her expression if he caught her eye. That's when she noticed the woman leaning against a navy blue BMW. It wasn't just the expensive car that was out of place. The woman was beautiful, elegant and...expensive. Her jeans were fitted, and obviously of good quality. She had on a short leather jacket to ward off the autumn chill and she wore sunglasses that must have cost more than Maggie earned in a week.

It was obvious that the woman was watching her, but Maggie had no idea why or even who she was.

"A friend of yours?" Molly asked, moving beside Maggie.

Lilly bounced her new baby as she moved to the other side of Maggie. "She looks angry," she commented as she patted her son's bottom, trying to keep him asleep.

Maggie didn't look away from the woman until her car disappeared out of the parking lot. "I've never seen her in my life," Maggie reported. "But I'm sure I don't like her."

"I don't either," Lilly muttered.

"She looks out of place," Molly replied, tilting her head slightly, mirroring Maggie's thought of just a moment ago. "And I don't think she likes you at all!"

"I got that impression," Maggie said, then shrugged as the woman's tail lights faded off down the road. "Whatever. Whoever she is, I've never met her and I have no idea why she was here." She turned around and smiled at her friends. "But I'm not letting her ruin this day. These girls have practiced long and hard. This is a great day for them!"

Lilly and Molly both agreed. "Drako ordered pizzas for everyone. It's all set up back at the apartments."

Maggie turned to her friend, her mouth falling open. "Are you kidding me?" she asked, staring at her friend with stunned excitement.

"Yep. I mentioned that this was the end of the season and he wanted to do something nice for the girls. So pizza party it is!"

"Excellent!" she said, then turned and made the announcement that there was a surprise back home.

The girls laughed and jumped up, more high fives were smacked around and Oliver lifted his hands in the air. "Everyone look around and pick up three pieces of trash!"

The girls moaned good naturedly, but they followed his order. They collected trash, bickering cheerfully about what constituted a proper piece of trash, and tossing their finds into either the recycling bin or the trashcan. They then set off for Rose Gardens Apartments, talking among themselves, eager for pizza.

Oliver held back, lugging the cooler over to his truck. He'd brought all of the equipment, so he'd driven himself and Maggie over instead of walking. "Who were you looking at a moment ago?" he asked, walking beside the three ladies.

Maggie squinted at the sunshine. "There was a woman. She seemed to be watching the game."

Lilly walked alongside them, still absently patting her son's bottom. "She was watching Maggie, Oliver. Not the game."

"She didn't look very nice," Molly mentioned.

"I agree," Maggie replied. "Have you heard anything from your friends down in Texas? Could that woman have anything to do with Jerry and the land? I haven't heard from him lately. So, I don't know what's going on."

"Jerry is a bit preoccupied just now," Oliver said, shoving the cooler back into his truck. Molly tossed the mesh bag filled with soccer balls in too, then stepped back. "He has a few legal issues to deal with."

"Legal issues?" Molly asked, surprised. "Is this...are you in trouble, Maggie?"

Maggie shook her head. "Not at all. Just...someone from my past came back, trying to intimidate me into doing something I don't want to do."

Lilly's hackles rose at that news. "Is this something that Drako could help with?" she asked, anger simmering in her blue eyes.

Maggie patted the newborn's back and shook her head. "Actually, Oliver made a few calls and, well, I haven't heard from him since. I thought he'd cause some trouble," she admitted, then felt Oliver's hands resting on her shoulders and smiled up at him. "But you did it. You got rid of that jerk."

"He was a putz, not a jerk," Oliver corrected. "Come on ladies. Let's go get some pizza."

By the time they arrived, the party was in full swing, with more pizzas being delivered even as they stepped out of their vehicles. "Looks like Drako went all out," Molly laughed, nudging Lilly's shoulder as they entered the courtyard where about sixty people were milling around, laughing and talking while eating pizza, drinking sodas, and there was even ice cold beer in a cooler off to one side, with Drako standing sentry, just in case one of the girls decided to be brave and try to sneak one.

He looked so intimidating standing there, but Maggie beamed at the terrifying man. Technically, she was his employee. But Drako treated her like his sister ever since he'd married Lilly. He treated Molly the same way and the three women loved him all the more for his protectiveness.

As soon as Lilly walked over, Drako took their son out of her arms and cradled the tiny infant against his chest. Maggie swallowed past the lump in her throat, wondering if she'd ever find a man that would be *that* in love with her.

She glanced at Oliver and was startled to find him staring back at her. And with the same longing in his eyes! Could he...? Was he...?

She banished the thought and looked away. That wasn't something she'd allow herself to hope for. Oliver was...well, he was temporary. She'd been burned once thinking that a man could love her. Jerry had crushed that hope under his arrogant heel.

Turning, she forced herself to smile as she made her way towards the tables that had been set up to hold the pizza boxes. There were still about six full pizzas left and she grabbed three plates, getting slices for Molly, Oliver, and Lilly.

When she brought them over to her friends, Molly and Oliver took their slices and eagerly bit into the cheesy treat. But Lilly shook her head, sliding her hand down over her plump stomach and hips. "Not for me," she told Maggie. "I'm still trying to lose this pregnancy weight."

There was an odd growling sound and Maggie looked up to find that Drako was scowling down at his wife. "Eat the pizza, love," he told her, a dark, dangerous look in his eyes. "Your figure is mine to watch, and I like it just the way it is."

A soft look passed between them. It was so intense, so filled with love and wonder that Maggie had to look away. Again, her gaze found

Oliver. And yes, he was still watching her. Maggie couldn't stop the sadness that enveloped her. She loved him so much. But…Maggie wasn't a loveable person. She was still trying. Still working to make up for her past life so that she could become the kind of woman that a man like Oliver could love.

Soon, she thought. Hopefully, she'd be worthy soon.

Oliver watched Maggie, his stomach aching at the pain he saw in her eyes. Why was she on the verge of tears? Because her friend was obviously madly in love with her husband?

Damn, he wanted to wrap his arms around her and tell her that he loved her that much. That he already was madly in love with her! But something held him back. Something told him that she was still wary. Why, he wasn't sure. But he'd get to her. He'd convince her that he loved her. Then they could find the same happiness that Lilly and the big guy had.

Speaking of the big guy, he looked vaguely familiar. When he found him across the courtyard, Oliver realized that the other man was watching him as well. Was he trying to place Oliver? Realizing that the other man might recognize him, Oliver moved to the pizza table, chatting with the girls' parents, putting several people between him and the other man. It wasn't that Oliver wanted to hide his identity exactly. But he wanted to hide his identity from Maggie. That comment she'd made a long time ago, about wealthy people being assholes, gave him pause.

Besides, he wanted Maggie to love him for himself. Not his bank account. He'd experienced the more mercenary side of "love" with Desiree. She hadn't cared for him as a person. She'd been more interested in what he could give her financially.

Maggie was the complete opposite. She had no idea that he was wealthy and powerful. It was a heady experience to know that she wanted him because of himself. Maggie wasn't motivated by money. She was motivated by kindness and generosity of spirit, which was new for him. He wanted something more pure and honest with Maggie.

But, if he wanted something pure and honest, why hadn't he told her about the development project? Honesty meant that he'd have to tell her who he really was and what he'd originally planned to do with the land and buildings in this area.

Not that he was moving forward with the project. Not anymore. He'd asked his development team to come up with more options, solutions that would help the entire neighborhood and not just the people that would eventually move in to the buildings that his company built. He wanted a more inclusive solution so that everyone profited. He'd lived here long enough to understand the hardships that inner city families struggled with every day. Oliver didn't want to come in and be yet another problem that pushed them further into jeopardy.

Wading back into the crowd, he watched and learned, listened and absorbed. Maggie considered herself to have been a brat over the years. But he might have hurt far more people than he realized. Thinking that, he made a mental note to go back to other projects, both current and finished, to measure the influence that his developments had on vulnerable communities. And if there was a negative impact, he was going to fix it.

Yes, his company was going to be a much more inclusive development company in the future.

"Why are you hiding over here?" Maggie asked as she sat beside him. He was over by the fire pit, hiding behind the evergreen trees she'd planted to add color to the area during the cold, grey months of winter. They also provided a nice backdrop to the spring and summer flowers, which made the whole area feel lush and inviting.

He took her hand and tugged her closer until their hips touched. "I'm not hiding," he explained. "Just sitting here, enjoying listening to the others."

Maggie smiled at him, wondering why she felt such a connection to this man in particular. "I have something to tell you, but I don't want to scare you away."

Immediately, she felt him pull away. She mentally kicked herself and wished that she'd kept her mouth shut.

"What's that?" he asked, standing up and moving to the other side of the fire pit.

Maggie pulled her legs up to her chest and wrapped her arms around them, shaking her head. "It's nothing. Nothing important."

From the look in his eyes, Oliver didn't believe her. Smart man!

"Maggie, if there's something you need to tell me, then just spit it out. I don't want any secrets from you."

Maggie sighed. "It wasn't anything important, Oliver. And I really don't want to mess up today. It's been really good between us for a while now. Let's just...leave it at that, okay?"

He glared at her. "Is that *really* what you want, Maggie? Are you honestly willing to settle for just okay?"

She cringed at his words as well as his tone, fear making her whole body turn cold. "Don't, Oliver," she whispered, her lips numb. "Just... I..."

"Maggie, damn it, you don't settle for anything less than perfection when it comes to managing these apartments," he snapped. He gestured around, encompassing the whole area. "Hell, you even manage the residents. They all adore you and you love them right back. You wouldn't settle for anything less than each and every one of them being deliriously happy, thriving, and loving life." He breathed in and closed his eyes. "So go ahead. Tell me. Just spit it out and let's not linger over the trivial stuff."

That really pissed her off and she uncurled her body and stood up. "Well, first of all, I consider you to be one of my friends as well. And you're right, I won't accept anything less than happiness for everyone, including you."

He opened his eyes and she could feel the anger in their depths. "So, tell me!"

Oliver knew the signs. She was about to break up with him. She'd been avoiding him all afternoon, so here it was.

"Fine! You want to know what I was going to say? Fine! But don't get mad if you don't like it."

"Maggie, just..."

"I like you, Oliver!" she interrupted, clearly steeling herself for... something. "Well, I did a few minutes ago. I was about to tell you how much I enjoyed being with you. That I like you and that you make me feel good! But now...now, I think I'll just head on home and let you... oomph!"

She couldn't finish because Oliver pulled her into his arms and kissed her. He didn't seem to care if anyone saw them like this. Oliver couldn't believe the relief he felt as she wrapped her arms around his neck and did that thing with his hair that he loved so much. It tickled and turned him on at the same time. And she was kissing him back! Damn, he loved it when she made those sexy little sounds when he kissed her!

When he lifted his head to look down at her, Oliver noticed that her lips were soft, full, and swollen. "I thought you were trying to break up with me," he admitted, his hands moving lower so that he was cupping her butt, gently pulling her closer so that she perfectly cradled his growing erection against her perfect hips.

Maggie blinked and he thought she looked so incredibly sexy like this. Or when she was naked. Or in the shower. Or standing in his doorway. Damn, he wanted to bring her back to his penthouse and make love to her in his huge bed, then cook something extravagant for her in his kitchen. He wanted to pour thousand dollar champagne over her soft curves, then wash her clean with his tongue, driving her just as wild as she did him.

"I wasn't." She whimpered when he ground his hips against hers, showing her just how turned on he was. Maggie licked her lips, her fingers teasing the nape of his neck again. "I was afraid to tell you how much you...how much you mean to me. I didn't want to scare you away."

He kissed her again, gently this time. "I'm not running away," he said, pointing out the obvious.

She beamed and Oliver wanted to roar with frustration. Because they were still out in the courtyard and he was so damned turned on, it would be a while before he could calm his body down enough to make it back to his apartment. But once he did, he was going to make love to her and show her just how much he liked her words. He was in love with her and she only liked him, but Oliver considered that progress. Damned fine progress!

Soon, he'd convince her they could make a go of this thing between them! He'd figure out how to turn her "like" into love and he'd make her so damn happy every day for the rest of her life!

Chapter 15

Desiree waited until the ugly blue pickup truck drove away. A pickup truck, she scoffed. Seriously? The always elegant, completely refined and reserved Oliver Fenton driving a pickup truck! Dear heaven, Desiree thought, shuddering with horror. How could he? The man had a beautiful Maserati and a Porsche. And he was driving around in a pathetic, rusty, old pickup. Ugh!

Tapping a finger on the steering wheel, she watched impatiently as the pickup drove down the street. Only when Oliver was well past the first stop light did she pull her beautiful BMW out of the church parking lot. It was the only place on this pathetic road that still had trees.

Driving down the road, she was grateful that it was early morning. She didn't like being in this part of the city. It was filthy and there were people sleeping in doorways a block away. Desiree knew that it was a community center or something and she made a mental note to send a donation to the charity. It never hurt to have one's name associated with places like that. Not that she'd ever enter the filthy place! Hell no!

Well, unless a reporter was doing a story about the community center! Desiree snickered, shaking her head at her hypocrisy. She didn't care one whit. She was a survivor and no one was going to pull her down! She had been raised a winner and damn it, she wanted Oliver! That man was the ultimate prize and would show the world that she'd won!

So, if this little snot of a woman was going to encroach on her man, Desiree considered it her mission to take the bitch down!

Pulling into the apartment complex, Desiree parked her BMW in a space far away from the other beaten up, dubious forms of transportation, looking around as she stepped out to make sure that no one was looking at her precious car.

She blipped the security system on and walked down the pathway between the buildings, determined to figure out where this woman lived and have a little chat with the bitch trying to steal her man.

But when she stepped through to the courtyard, Desiree stopped, stunned by the beauty in front of her. The lush landscaping surrounded a quaint, beautifully built fire pit area, the inviting benches calling to her to take a seat and relax. It was...unexpected, given the harshness of the surrounding area.

Then she looked around a bit more. The interior courtyard of the buildings looked clean and freshly painted. The doors had a new coat of paint on them as well and...actually, the doors looked new! Good grief, she turned and looked back through the two buildings that formed a V and looked out to the parking lot again. Sure enough, the concrete jungle mixed with a tangle of electrical and telephone wires was still there.

But this courtyard...was beautiful! It was literally an oasis of beauty nestled within one of the worst parts of town.

Shaking off her surprise, she turned, her lips pressing into a determined expression once again. Glancing towards the entrance, she spotted the manager's office. It looked like just another apartment, but the sign on the door announced that it was the manager's space, so she stomped over to it. A sharp knock on the door didn't result in anyone appearing in front of her. So she rapped again, harder this time.

"Can I help you?" someone asked from behind her.

Desiree spun around, startled to find her prey standing innocently on the sidewalk, her green eyes sparkling and...well, they were very pretty eyes, she thought. Desiree had only seen this woman from a distance and thought that she'd been...merely average. But up close, the woman really was quite lovely, in a soft, unsophisticated way.

Desiree sniffed. Oliver didn't need this...woman. He didn't need "pretty". He needed gorgeous! And Desiree was that woman! She was the one who could help Oliver's career. Not this...pipsqueak, upstart, irritatingly nice woman. No, "nice" simply wouldn't do. Nice people were crushed in this town. The power hungry people who lived and worked in Washington DC scraped "nice" off of their shoe after stomping it into the ground!

Oliver needed someone stronger. More capable of taking on the power-hungry freaks that ruled this town.

"I'm Desiree Milken," she said, extending her hand. "I'm Oliver Fenton's fiancée. And you are?" she asked, using that silky tone that she'd perfected over the years.

Obviously, her tone worked if the startled pain in the woman's eyes was any indication.

Maggie stared up at the tall, elegantly beautiful woman. Her false eye-lashes made her eyes look huge and the perfectly applied makeup gave the impression of movie-star glamour. Her hair was thick and lush, cascading over her shoulder in shimmering waves. She wasn't wearing normal jeans ether. Nope, those were designer jeans that fit her pain-fully thin body like a glove. Her leather boots had four inch heels and the sweater was obviously cashmere. In other words, this woman came from money!

Maggie recognized the signs of money. She also recognized the signs of a lie. A mere two weeks ago, Jerry had come back into her life and announced that he was Maggie's fiancé. A complete lie and Oliver had been furious until Maggie had explained.

This woman was obviously trying to do the same thing, but Maggie had grown to understand Oliver better over these past few weeks.

With that realization, Maggie's pain subsided and she shook her head, crossing her arms over her chest. "No, you're not," Maggie replied, tilting her head slightly. The tightening of the woman's lips confirmed her suspicions. "Oliver is a man of integrity."

"You don't think that Oliver and I–"

Maggie lifted a hand, stopping her lies. She was pulling on her past experience as a spoiled brat, which was exactly what this woman seemed to be. Maggie examined this Desiree Milken and wondered if she'd come across this arrogant and demeaning when she'd lived down in Texas. Probably, she sighed, accepting yet another facet of herself that she didn't like.

Straightening her spine, she lifted her chin. That arrogant, pathetic, spoiled brat was in the past. She was better now. She was a stronger, kinder, more generous person!

"I believe that you and Oliver may have been engaged at some point," she interrupted. The flash in the woman's eyes conveyed Maggie was right on target. "But you're not anymore. Which means you're here to cause problems. Why?"

The woman breathed in slowly, her eyes glaring daggers at Maggie.

"You're not right for Oliver," Desiree snapped. "Oliver needs someone by his side who can help him. Someone who can further his career and ensure that he meets the right people."

Maggie bristled at that assertion. "Since coming here, I've helped Oli-ver," she stated firmly. "Oliver was down on his luck and sinking fast. I gave him a place to live and..."

The woman's harsh laughter stopped Maggie's defense. "You think that Oliver lives *here*?" she sneered, gesturing to the quaint, but small, apartments. "Oh, honey!" The woman's condescending tone and shake of her head warned Maggie that she wasn't going to like what she said next. "You have no idea who Oliver Fenton *is*, do you?"

"I know Oliver," Maggie said firmly. "He's a good man. And he's strong."

A snort told Maggie that something was definitely amiss. "Yeah," she said, nodding her head. "He's strong. And powerful. But he doesn't live here," she continued with another snort. "Oliver Fenton is the CEO of Fenton Companies. He's the CEO of a freaking empire! Plus, he comes from a wealthy, powerful family!"

Maggie heard the words, but it took her a moment to process them. Oliver was...a CEO? But how could that be? He'd been looking for a place to sleep in an abandoned building! His dirty clothes, the scruff of his beard! She'd seen the signs before. Oliver had been struggling!

"Furthermore, Oliver lives in a beautiful penthouse that looks out over the city, right on the edge of the Potomac River." The woman looked pointedly around, shaking her head sadly. "No, Oliver might be slumming around here, but that's only because he has a plan. He's working an angle and..." she froze and frowned. Obviously, she'd just figured something out and her face paled dramatically beneath the expertly applied makeup.

Desiree nervously gripped the strap of her expensive, leather purse and almost tripped over her feet as she turned towards the exit. "I have to go," she mumbled, already striding away.

Maggie watched bemused, as the woman practically ran to her car. Now she was thoroughly confused. What in the world had caused this malicious woman to just run off like that?

Maggie replayed the conversation in her mind. "Slumming?" she whispered, hurt that the woman would refer to her precious, beautiful community as a slum! And a CEO? "Oliver is a construction worker!" she muttered emphatically, turning to look at his apartment. They'd spent a great deal of time over the past week finalizing the details in his apartment.

Granted, she hadn't asked Oliver to sign a lease agreement. If she had, Maggie might have gotten his employment information. And his last name. And maybe his salary information. Good grief, had she been a complete idiot?!

"I didn't want to embarrass him," she whispered as her only defense, ducking her head. But deep down inside, in her heart and in her brain, Maggie had sort of suspected that Oliver was more than what he seemed. Was he really a wealthy businessman? Or was he the down-on-his-luck construction worker, looking for a place to live?

Thinking back to that morning, Maggie remembered thinking how strong he clearly was. She'd been right. Maggie was intimately aware of Oliver's strength. So if he'd been homeless, how had he honed those muscles?

She walked over to one of the benches, but couldn't focus enough to sit down, her mind reeling. Thinking back, there had been clues. The new soccer balls and soccer equipment. Had it all really been a gift from his employer? Or had Oliver simply gone out and bought the equipment himself?

Then there were the ice cream bars after the final game. And all of the supplies for the renovation he'd done in his apartment. The tiles, the fancy faucet, the flooring...those things weren't cheap!

And that hurt! Goodness, it hurt a lot. She loved Oliver. But who did she really love? The man she thought he was? And who was that, really?

"Maggie?" Molly called out walking down the stairs from her apartment. But when Molly spotted Maggie, her friend rushed over and grabbed Maggie under the arm. "What's wrong? What just happened? Did that woman say something to upset you?" Molly breathed in and shook her head. "What am I saying? Obviously, she did. Sorry, that was a ridiculous question." She led Maggie over to one of the benches. "Okay, sit down and tell me what happened."

Maggie looked around, still stunned from the news. "Umm....she said something about being Oliver's fiancé at first, but," her hand flew to cover her mouth and Maggie breathed in slowly, trying to steady her nerves. "She lied. I *know* she lied about that."

Molly snorted. "Of course she lied. Oliver wouldn't be with you if he was engaged. That's a fact!"

Maggie nodded, a sort of numbness taking the place of the waves of pain. "Yeah. That's almost exactly what I told her. Then she admitted that they had been engaged and would be again. She said Oliver needed a wife that..." she closed her eyes, swallowing hard past the lump in her throat. "Well, she said that Oliver needed a wife that could handle his lifestyle."

Another inelegant snort. "You can definitely handle Oliver's lifestyle. Good grief, just look at how you two brought the girls' soccer team into first place last week! The girls came in last in the spring tournament."

Maggie closed her eyes, rubbing her forehead slightly. "Yeah. He's a great coach." She realized what she'd just said, another piece of the puzzle falling into place. Another clue that Maggie had ignored! "He's a good leader. He's a natural leader."

Molly nodded firmly. "Exactly. You'd thought he was in the military. Maybe he was an officer?"

Maggie cringed visibly at the reminder of how badly she'd misread the situation. "Can I see your phone?" she asked.

Molly immediately dug it out and handed it over. Maggie did a Google search. Sure enough, as soon as she typed in the name "Oliver Fenton", Oliver's wonderful, handsome face popped up. And underneath that wonderful face was the name, "Oliver Fenton, CEO of Fenton Companies, a Global Property Development Firm headquartered in Washington, D.C."

"Wow!" Molly whispered, reading over Maggie's shoulders. "He looks hot in a suit!"

Molly was right, but what did that mean? Why had Oliver been looking around next door in the empty apartments? Maggie had assumed Oliver had been searching for a place to shelter overnight. But what if there was more to it than that? What if Oliver...! An icy sensation settled into the pit of her stomach.

"I need to go," Maggie whispered, returning the phone.

"Where are you going?" Molly asked, shoving the phone back into her pocket and standing up as Maggie raced across the courtyard to her apartment. She didn't reply, but simply pushed through the door, grabbed her purse and car keys, then ran to her beat up old sedan.

She drove for a few minutes in stupid, stunned silence, but then Maggie knew what she had to do. Pulling over into a grocery store parking lot, she pulled up the address for Fenton Companies. With dread, Maggie put the address into her GPS app. The building was only four miles away!

Chapter 16

"No, I don't have time for Desiree right now," Oliver snapped as he headed down the hall to his next meeting. Jamie struggled to keep up, but he was about a foot shorter than Oliver and looked frazzled. Which was another reason why he didn't want to deal with Desiree today. The woman was really getting on his nerves!

"But sir, she…" Jamie paused and picked up his cell phone. "Yes?" Oliver ignored his assistant and kept walking, stepping into the conference room and nodding to the people already gathered there. Jamie followed, still nodding even though the meeting was scheduled to start. "Yes. Okay. No, I don't recognize the name." More nodding, then Jamie covered the phone. "There is a woman down in the lobby asking to speak with you."

"Get rid of her," Oliver snapped, then sat down at the head of the long, polished table and nodded. "Let's go."

Jamie sat down as well, but the phone buzzed and he checked the message. *"Woman says that Oliver Fenton will be evicted if she doesn't speak with him."* Jamie re-read the message, trying to understand the words because they were simply too insane.

With a sigh, Jamie stood up and left the room, knowing that he'd have to make the determination to have the woman arrested or just evicted from the building.

When he stepped out of the elevator on the ground floor, he spotted the woman easily enough. She was the only one in the building wearing jeans. She was also lovely. Those green eyes were beautiful and… angry! Her long, brown hair cascaded over her shoulder from a high ponytail, showcasing her delicate cheekbones. The woman was incredibly lovely! And unable to hold still. She was pacing the lobby, muttering to herself.

"Ms. Beauchamp?" he asked.

"Yes," the pretty woman who, upon closer inspection, was truly beautiful, extended her hand politely. "I'm Maggie Beauchamp," she replied with a tone that spoke of calm control at great cost. "I need to speak with Oliver Fenton for a moment, if you don't mind. We have some personal business that needs to be discussed in private."

"I'm sorry, but Mr. Fenton is in a meeting. May I take a message for him?"

The pretty woman gulped and blinked back tears, seeming to deflate with resignation. Jamie watched the woman for a long moment. She appeared to be coming to terms with something, but Jamie had no idea what that "something" was.

Finally, her shoulders drooped and she shook her head. "No. No message." She turned away, but after only a few steps, she turned back to him. "Actually, yes. Please tell Oliver that..." she closed her eyes and took a deep breath. "Tell him Maggie needs his apartment keys back. Tell him that I'll ensure that he's reimbursed for the materials, as well as his time and effort. He'll know what that means."

With that, she headed towards the doors again. Something about the way she carried herself whispered to Jamie that she was struggling with very strong emotions. Plus, the message...it didn't make sense. Except that Jamie knew that there had been something very odd going on with his boss over the past several weeks.

"Ms. Beauchamp!" Jamie called out, his instincts kicking in. When the woman stopped, but didn't turn around, his gut twisted alarmingly, warning him that something was very wrong.

"Why don't you come with me?" he offered. "Mr. Fenton should be out of his meeting in a few minutes and I'm sure that he can spare you a moment."

The woman was still for a long moment, obviously mentally debating the issue. Thankfully, in the end, she nodded sharply. Jamie led the way to the elevators and they went up to the executive floor in silence.

"This way," Jamie explained, leading her down the long, plush hallway towards Oliver's office. If this truly was a personal issue, Oliver probably wouldn't want it announced to the world. But at the last minute, Jamie decided to put the woman in one of the executive conference rooms instead of Oliver's office. He didn't know why, but he wanted to protect Oliver's privacy.

"You can wait in here," Jamie said, opening the door to one of the larger conference rooms. "Can I get you some coffee or tea? Juice or a soda, perhaps?"

Maggie looked around, impressed despite her anger. The short man was staring at her as if expecting her to shatter into a zillion pieces. He wasn't far off!

"No. Thank you. I'm fine," she finally replied, then moved deeper into the conference room. It was a nice room with a brightly polished table and expensive, black leather chairs with high backs. It was a power room, she thought, recognizing the effort. A room used to intimidate and impress.

It worked. Maggie was definitely impressed and intimidated. She rubbed sweaty palms down over her worn jeans, wishing that she'd taken the time to change into a dress. Or maybe a suit. Anything that might help her to feel a bit less intimidated. More as if she belonged in this world.

At one point, she would have felt perfectly comfortable in a room like this. Maggie would have assumed that she had every right to a room like this. She would have felt on top of the world to have been shown to this room.

Now, Maggie just wanted to get out of here.

"This was a bad idea," she muttered, pulling her purse higher onto her shoulder as she turned to leave, determined to get out of here and talk to Oliver later tonight. There had to be an explanation. It was silly to confront him like this. Silly and petty.

Maggie was reaching for the doorknob when the door pushed open and she jumped back.

"Oh!" a guy yelped, startled himself. "Sorry about that!" he laughed. He pulled a cart into the room that had a miniature mock-up of a city on it. "I wasn't aware that anyone would be in here this early. I was just told to deliver his mock up to this conference room." He pulled the cart up to the table and hefted one half of the "city" onto the conference room table, then the second half. He carefully adjusted the halves so that they were perfectly aligned.

"Isn't this just incredible?" the man gushed, bending down to make sure that the parts were perfectly placed. "This part of Crystal City is a dump! But Mr. Fenton has plans to make over the whole area! He has several options. This is just the first. But it's my favorite." He chuckled, shaking his head, clearly in awe. "I mean, imagine buying up old buildings and land so that we can replace those decrepit dumps with new, fresh designs that can offer so much more to everyone! It's just genius!"

Maggie stared, unable to respond as she looked down at the diorama of her neighborhood. She'd spotted Rose Gardens Apartments easily enough because of the courtyard. Someone had taken great pains to make this mockup as real as possible.

"These babies cost a few thousand dollars to create, but Mr. Fenton prefers to visualize the options," the guy explained, resting his hands on his hips. "Okay, I need to go get the other two options and get them set up too. I'll be right back."

He disappeared out the door, leaving Maggie alone. Alone with the truth of Oliver's betrayal.

It wasn't that he was engaged. It wasn't that he was a powerful man who had more money than god!

No, Oliver's betrayal was that he was going to destroy her world. Literally! Looking closely at the diorama, she spotted the place where the community center, where Molly worked and the residents gathered ...used to stand. In its place was a sky rise, with retail shops and restaurants on the bottom floor, several levels of office space and, from the small descriptions alongside each building, condominiums on the top floors. It was perhaps thirty stories high, but that wasn't the tallest building around. Nope, there were four more buildings. The other three rose up over the shops and small, family owned restaurants that dotted the landscape of the neighborhood. The apartment complex next to Rose Gardens was gone, replaced by condos six floors high. There was a price tag on the condos in that building's description and Maggie gasped at the amount. Surely no one would pay *that* much for a one or two bedroom home that didn't even come with its own butler!

She continued to examine the mockup, pain lashing at her as she searched for the soccer field. It was gone. Several of the high-rise buildings took up the area where her precious neighborhood used to be. Maggie suspected that the base of the buildings needed to be wider than the current city block in order to sustain the weight of thirty or forty floors.

Maggie's hand flew up to smother a sob. She couldn't look any longer. Turning, she rushed out of the conference room, practically running down the hallway. She pressed the button for the elevator, then waited impatiently for several people to exit before she stepped in.

For several, painful moments, she waited, fighting to keep her face still and her eyes from leaking. Finally, the elevator opened and, since Maggie was in the back, she waited while the others filed out. But when she finally had a pathway, she rushed out of the elevator, apologizing when she accidentally bumped people in her haste to get away.

When she finally reached her car, which had been parked in the underground parking garage, she felt as if she might just explode from the pain. "Not yet," she told herself firmly. "Just wait until you get out of here!"

It was a short trip back home, but when she reached the familiar streets of her neighborhood, something else occurred to her. Instead of heading to her home, she drove the extra block to the community center. Sure enough, Molly was outside, plucking apples from the trees and waved cheerfully when Maggie pulled into a parking space.

But as soon as Molly saw her friend's face drenched in tears, Molly dropped her basket and rushed to comfort Maggie.

"What happened? What did he say? Is he truly engaged?" Molly asked, enveloping Maggie in a tight hug and holding her still.

"Worse!" Maggie whispered through the pain. She squeezed her eyes closed as Molly's arms tightened around her.

"Okay, we'll figure this out, together. Let's go to my office. I'll call Lilly and we'll figure this out together."

Maggie nodded, wiping away her tears with her hands and wishing that she had a tissue.

Finally, they ended up in Molly's tiny conference room, since her office was too small. Molly parked Maggie on the worn, pleather couch, and handed her a box of tissues. "Okay, start talking. What's going on?"

Maggie wiped her eyes and blew her nose, then tossed the tissue into the trash and took another. "Remember those rumors about someone buying up the vacant properties around the neighborhood?"

Molly shrugged, but at the look in Maggie's eyes, she stopped. "No!"

"Yes," Maggie replied. "Apparently, the new owner of this neighborhood is none other than Oliver Fenton." She laughed, shaking her head, "Actually, it's Fenton Companies, one of which is Fenton Development and Fenton Properties. There are numerous other companies, but they all revolve around buying up large parcels of land with the intent of tearing down the entire neighborhood, so they can make room for thirty and forty story buildings."

"*No!*"

"Yep!" Maggie confirmed, squeezing her eyes shut for a moment. "I just came from Oliver's office. And yes, he's in charge. Not the son or the soon to be owner or anything like that. He's the genius behind all of it. And I saw the layout." She sniffed again. "Wanna know what's going here?"

Molly looked around at the messy but comfortable conference room, then back to Maggie. "Here? What do you mean?"

"I mean," she sniffed again, "Oliver plans on putting boutique stores here. And a restaurant. Wouldn't it be hilarious if there was a Tiffany's in this spot? Or maybe a Bergdorf's?"

Molly stared at Maggie, slowly shaking her head. "No. I don't think that would be all that amusing."

Maggie hiccupped and took another tissue. "Yeah, I guess not."

Chapter 17

"Why did you let Desiree in here??" Oliver demanded, storming into his office but...sighing and...coming to a halt when he realized that Desiree was already there.

Jamie glowered. "She must have slipped through when I was downstairs. Sir, a woman came by to see you. But she's gone now."

Desiree wasn't waiting around. She rushed forward, ignoring Jamie.

"I didn't mean to spill your secrets, Oliver," she blurted. "I didn't know that she wasn't aware of who you were!"

A very bad feeling washed over Oliver all of a sudden. "What are you talking about?" he demanded, tossing the reports from his last meeting onto his desk. He was tired and hungry. All he wanted to do was head out of here and find Maggie.

"Maggie," Desiree said.

That got his attention and he stiffened angrily. "What about Maggie?" he demanded.

"I didn't know that she wasn't aware of who you were, Oliver!"

His jaw clenched. "So you took it upon yourself to fill her in?" he asked, his voice deadly soft.

Oliver was already halfway to the door when her words registered.

"How was I supposed to know that she didn't know who you were? You're huge in this town! She's an idiot if she didn't...!"

"Stop it, Desiree! What did you do? Why would she find out now?"

She shrank back and he wanted to roar with fury.

"She was just spouting something about...well, how good you were and all of that silliness about...whatever. I laughed and then realized that you must be there in the apartment complex in order to find out information about the neighborhood," she rushed to explain. "I understand now. You were just doing research, using her to find out more

102

about the neighborhood. It's actually genius, Oliver," she continued. "I mean, to pretend to be in love with someone just to get information on your next project?" Desiree laughed, shrugging. "But I didn't let that cat out of the bag. When I realized what you were doing, that you were only there as a spy, sort of, I left. I doubt she realized what was going on. I didn't tell her and there's no way she could possibly know about your plans."

Oliver glared at Desiree, wishing that he could fire her. But that thought was banished when Jamie sighed.

"She knows," his assistant announced, staring at his shoes.

Oliver's head swung around to glare at Jamie. "She knows *what*?"

Jamie cringed, pulling his notebook closer to his chest. "Maggie Beauchamp came by earlier today," Jamie explained.

Oliver stared. "Here?" he demanded. "Maggie was here?"

Jamie cringed. "Yes?"

Oliver's eyes hardened. "Is that an answer or a question?" he demanded softly.

Jamie's shoulders slumped. "Maggie Beauchamp was here. I didn't know who she was. But...well, there was something about the way she presented herself to the security team downstairs that indicated that she was important to you. So, I slipped out of that meeting right before noon. I brought her up here, but because I didn't know who she was, I didn't want to put her in your office." He turned to glare at Desiree. "I've been doing an excellent job of keeping the undesirables out of your office, sir."

Desiree barely sniffed at the insult because she knew that she'd messed up big time.

"So, if you knew that she was important to me, why didn't you come and get me? I would have paused the meeting for Maggie."

"What?" Desiree practically screeched.

Oliver sighed. "I love Maggie, Desiree. She's very important to me. So just let that information sink in while Jamie finishes what he's trying to tell me."

"But you were engaged to *me!*" she blurted, stepping forward. But when Oliver shot a quelling glance her way, Desiree took an involuntary step backwards.

"Jamie, continue. Where is Maggie?"

"She left," Jamie explained. "When I came back to the conference room with coffee for her, she was gone. Matt in development was there, setting up the options for that new project that you mentioned. And...?"

Jamie stopped when Oliver sliced his hand through the air. "Are you telling me that Maggie saw the plans? That she was there?" He barely waited until Jamie nodded confirmation before he demanded, "Which plans did she see?"

Jamie shrugged. "I don't know. When I came back the second time, Matt was setting up option two, and option one was already on the table. It's the most impressive, so I don't see how the plans could have bothered her."

Oliver cursed under his breath as he grabbed his car keys off and hurried out of his office.

"What about me?" Desiree called out.

He ignored her. All he knew was that he had to get to Maggie. He had to explain. He couldn't imagine what might be going through her mind.

Correction, he was pretty sure that he did know what was going through her mind. That he'd lied to her. That he'd tricked her. But Oliver knew that he'd never actively lied to her.

He didn't think that she'd believe him. Or maybe he hadn't told her the truth, which was a lie of omission. That wasn't as bad, was it?

Damn it, rush hour traffic was horrendous. Washington, D.C. traffic was bad enough that even the five miles from his office to the apartments meant a forty-five minute drive that was more like sitting in a parking lot.

Finally, he reached the turnoff for the apartment and zoomed down the street. He slowed down as he pulled into the parking lot, cautious because the kids played in the parking lot after school and before they were called in for dinner.

As he stepped out of his car, he noticed that Maggie's wasn't in her usual spot. Was she not here? But if she wasn't, where would she be?

He hurried to her apartment door and unlocked it. They'd traded keys a couple of weeks ago. But when he walked through the apartment, calling for her, there was no response. Just silence.

Silence was bad! Every night for the past few weeks, Maggie had been here, waiting for him when he returned from work. Granted, he was early tonight, since he would normally go to his penthouse and change into jeans, but still, she'd been here. Excited to see him and he'd been just as thrilled!

But there was no Maggie.

When he stepped out of the apartment, looking around, he found Eddie and Mick standing by the fire pit. Both were glaring daggers at him. Instantly, Oliver knew that word had spread.

"Do you know where Maggie is?" he asked politely.

Mick shook his head. Eddie glared harder. "You're just gonna tear down the neighborhood. We're not telling you nothing."

Oliver sighed, rubbing the back of his neck as fear of losing Maggie hit him hard. "I'm not going to tear anything down," he told them, ignoring their obvious surprise. "In fact, she only saw one of the options. The plan I'm going with is much more inclusive. My company owns almost all of the land around here now. But I think there's a way that we can make this whole area a lot nicer to live in, without tearing down anything." He backed up. "If you see Maggie, will you tell her that? Will you tell her that I'm not tearing anything down?"

The men didn't answer, but Oliver saw the look in their eyes. They were good men and wanted Maggie to be happy. They'd tell her.

But four hours later, he walked into his penthouse, defeated. He still hadn't found Maggie. Everywhere he'd gone, people had glared and yelled at him. They thought he was the devil about to destroy their neighborhood.

He showered and stretched out on his bed, staring at the ceiling. The bed was too soft, he thought. And the room too big. It felt cavernous after sleeping in the cozy apartment with Maggie for so long. And Maggie wasn't here. Oliver realized that nothing felt right without Maggie.

Chapter 18

Maggie opened her eyes and sighed. Another miserable day. Another day without Oliver. Another day wondering how she'd been so gullible. First Jerry, then Oliver. Both had thought she was stupid enough to trick her into thinking they wanted her. When in reality, they only wanted what she could give them. Jerry wanted the land. Oliver wanted information on the neighborhood.

"Oh, good! You're awake!" Lilly laughed as she stepped into the bedroom, Marcus gurgling happily in her arms. "Here, hold him for me for a minute, would you?" she asked, handing over the cooing child, and rushing out of the room.

Maggie stared down into Marcus' face, fighting back the tears. She loved kids. If things had gone the way she'd hoped, then she and Oliver would have had a whole passel of children.

Alas, Maggie suspected she'd never have that wonderful brood. She couldn't imagine ever trusting a man again. Jerry's betrayal had been painful enough. But she'd come through that trial better and stronger.

Oliver's betrayal...well, he'd nearly destroyed her.

"No more!" she whispered to the adorable baby boy, who squirmed and giggled at her. "Never again!"

Marcus bicycled his tiny feet harder, giggling excitedly. Maggie laughed as she set him down in the middle of the bed, and slipped out of bed to get dressed.

When Lilly returned, her eyes widened. "Something changed," she announced, scooping Marcus out of Maggie's arms. "What's happened?"

"I'm going back," she declared.

Lilly shook her head. "No! You're staying here until you feel better." She started patting Marcus' bottom, soothing him as she swayed slightly. "You've lost too much weight and I know you're still not sleeping well."

"I'm fine," Maggie insisted, feeling a rush of warmth for her friends. Molly came over every day with cookies or treats from Louise and Nora, or clothes from her apartment. She also provided the news that Oliver was still living at Rose Gardens. Which was very odd, since Maggie had Googled his penthouse. It was beautiful! Huge and clean, white and pristine! His penthouse was nothing like the one bedroom place at Rose Gardens.

"You need to stay here," she repeated.

Maggie hugged her friend, and kissed Marcus' soft, fluffy head. "I have to get to work. There are apartments that need work. Things to do and people who need me. I'm not running away like I did with Jerry."

Lilly continued patting Marcus' bottom as she said, "Speaking of jerks, I have some news about Jerry."

Maggie pulled out the duffel bag Molly had packed for her, stuffing clothes in haphazardly. Funny, but the thought of Jerry didn't hurt anymore. How long would it be before she could say the same about Oliver? "What about him?"

"Well, you know how Drako owns several businesses down in Houston, including a bank, and..."

"Drako owns a bank?" Maggie interrupted, surprised by that little tidbit.

Lilly waved it aside. "Yes, but that's not the interesting part. Apparently, Jerry has gone to several banks now, asking for loans." She grinned, a sparkle in her eyes. "It appears that dear old Jerry is broke." Lilly grinned. "Worse than broke. He has bill collectors calling on him constantly."

"Really?" Maggie asked, laughing as she collected her socks.

"Yep. He mortgaged his house and his ranch to buy up all of your land around the river. Now that the developer has mysteriously pulled out, Jerry is left with a massive debt, and no one wants to buy that land. He's even trying to sell it dirt cheap. But...wonder of wonders, whenever he gets a nibble of interest, the buyer mysteriously pulls out."

"Why is that?" she asked.

Lilly shrugged. "Apparently, there's a big developer down there warning people away from the sale. The land is cursed or something, people are whispering."

Maggie stopped packing, looking at her friend. "Cursed?" she repeated. "And what developer?"

"Fenton properties, is what Drako heard." She shrugged, as if the news was of little import.

Maggie caught her breath. "Oliver is doing this to Jerry? But...why?"

Another shrug. "No clue. Maybe he's trying to make up for what he thinks he's done here?"

Maggie shoved the last sweater into the duffel bag. "Not a chance!" she spat.

Lilly followed, bouncing Marcus with every step. "Well, I'm just saying that there might be more going on than we know. It's possible that Oliver might not be as horrible as you think."

Maggie turned, her eyes narrowing on her friend. "What do you know?"

Lilly smiled. "A little birdie told me the neighborhood is getting a major revitalization grant from the state. And there are several developers trying to step in and spruce up the apartments around Rose Gardens." She swayed again. "Oh, and...there's some politician who found out about the Center and is asking questions. But that might be just a rumor."

"A politician?"

Lilly grinned. "Yeah, the rumors are that someone is running for a weakened senator's seat. That pathetic senator is my father, by the way." She laughed and did a little spin, thrilled by any bad news regarding her corrupt father. "Gossip about some handsome lawyer-guy is spreading around town and...well, you should ask Molly about that. She hates him, but I think he's pretty charming."

Maggie eyed her friend dubiously. "If Molly hates this guy, then we shouldn't trust him. She has an excellent instinct for people."

Lilly laughed. "I'm not so sure if her instincts are on point about this guy." Lilly shrugged slightly. "I also think that you should talk to Oliver. There has to be more to his story than we know."

Maggie's eyes narrowed on her friend. "Are you on his side now?"

Lilly shook her head. "I'm on *your* side. I just want you to think about every possibility before you reject a man who might be your soul mate. Don't lose something that could be precious, just because you've been hurt."

Maggie understood. Lilly had loved Drako from the beginning, but he didn't believe he could love again. Thankfully, they'd worked things out and were wildly happy and, now they were crazy about their little boy.

Maggie smiled gently and leaned in to hug her friend. "I love you for wanting me to find the same happiness that you have with Drako, but I don't think that's in my future."

And with that, she slung her duffel over her shoulder. "I'm truly grateful to you for giving me a place to stay over the past few days." She placed another kiss on Marcus' sweet-smelling head. "I'll talk to you soon."

Chapter 19

Oliver was going to spank Maggie's ass as soon as he found her. In the meantime, he ran a hand through his hair, scanning the horizon in the hope that he'd see her. Unfortunately, Maggie still hadn't returned. Molly assured him that Maggie was safe, but that she was also hurt and confused. He'd tried to convince Molly that he'd messed up. Molly had simply told him to be patient.

"Right!" he snapped, turning back to the architect, who was taking measurements. Patience wasn't in great supply just now. He'd be more patient if he could just talk to Maggie, explain to her what had happened.

Three days! She'd been gone for three days! It felt more like three years. He barely slept, hated eating without Maggie smiling across the table, and he struggled to focus on work when all he really wanted was Maggie in his arms.

Yeah, he'd messed up. But not in the way she thought.

An hour later, he was leaving the Center when he spotted a man that looked vaguely familiar standing in front of the building. "Can I help you?" he asked, instantly alert and curious.

The man pulled off his sunglasses. "James Morgan," the man said, extending his hand with an easy smile. "And you're Oliver Fenton, correct?"

Oliver liked him at once. It didn't hurt that the man's reputation as a determined and hardworking legal genius preceded him. The man had won some pretty amazing lawsuits over the years.

"That's right. James Morgan. You're running for Senator Von Deuch's seat this time around, aren't you?"

"That's me," the guy replied. "I was just–" he stopped, his eyes focusing on something over Oliver's shoulder. Oliver turned, following his gaze. Molly came around the corner, laughing as she ran full out with something in her arms. About three seconds later, a stream of kids galloped after her. Oliver chuckled softly when Molly spun around, hiding behind a tree. It wasn't a good move, because those kids were street smart. They surrounded her without mercy. Within moments, the kids had her on the ground, cheering with their success.

Molly emerged from the dog pile, laughing and tossing her curly ponytail over her shoulder as she stood up. "Okay!" she laughed. "You win!" The object in her hands was a box of popsicles that she immediately began handing out to eat.

"That's Molly," Oliver offered. "She's the director here at the Center." He looked at the man who appeared to be too stunned to speak. "Would you like an introduction?"

The man continued to stare. Then slowly, as if still entranced, he nodded. "Yes please!"

Oliver chuckled. "I know the feeling," he said, having experienced that same kind of lightning bolt when he'd first laid eyes on Maggie.

And that's when he saw her. She was getting out of her car. She looked around, obviously looking for Molly, but spotted him first. He saw her stiffen and knew that she was considering getting back into her car. Thankfully, she decided against it.

It wouldn't matter. Not this time. He would have followed her. And he would have caught her. Maggie was just too important for him to lose again.

"Sorry buddy," he told James, patting him on the back. "You're on your own. I have an important mission."

The other man might have nodded, or he could have started doing cartwheels. Oliver had no clue since his attention was focused on Maggie.

"What are you doing here?" she asked as he reached her.

"Waiting for you," he admitted honestly. "I knew that you'd come back here eventually."

Maggie sighed, disconcerted because she hadn't expected Oliver to be here. She knew that they needed to talk, if only so that she could get the keys to his apartment back. But she didn't like confrontations. Not like this.

"Well, are you moving out?"

"Nope," he replied, taking her arm and leading her over to an area that was partially hidden by a group of bushes, giving them some privacy. "I'm not leaving, Maggie. And you're going to listen to me."

"I am?" she demanded, glaring up at him.

Damn, he loved her spunk. "Yes. You are. This isn't what you think."

She folded her arms protectively over her stomach and glared at him. "So, you didn't buy up all of the properties in an eight or nine block area with the intention of tearing it all down and building sky rises?"

He rubbed the back of his neck. "Okay, so yeah. That part is right. As far as it goes."

"And you didn't inhabit that apartment with the intention of getting information out of me?"

"No!" he replied forcefully, shaking his head. "Absolutely not. I didn't move into that apartment to spy on you or anyone else."

"You just wanted to slum around for a while? Ignoring your luxurious penthouse? Which is ugly by the way!" she told him. "I looked it up online. The decorator you chose needs to add more color to their designs. The place looks like a morgue."

He chuckled. "Because you've been inside so many morgues lately?"

Her eyes narrowed. "Point made, but your penthouse is still cold and soulless."

"I agree," he replied easily. "That's why I put it on the market."

That surprised her. She blinked and her lips moved, but she didn't speak for a moment. "Why?"

"Because I realized it wasn't what I wanted. And because I didn't think that you'd like living there."

Her mouth fell open and he knew that he had her now.

"You're right," she rallied, looking away. "I wouldn't like living there. Especially because *you* live there."

"No, I live two doors down from you. And maybe," he moved closer, "if you'll listen to me, maybe we could find a place to move into, together."

She'd stiffened at his softer tone, but when he finished that suggestion, Maggie was already shaking her head. "No! Not gonna happen. I don't trust you."

He sighed, nodding his understanding. "I know that. And I'll work on earning your trust back. But Maggie, I didn't move into the apartment to spy on you. That move was only to get to know you better. Although, I'll admit that moving in with you and getting to know the residents around here, did change my plans for the neighborhood."

Maggie snorted. She was losing the battle and wanted to step back. But he took her hand instead. "Will you come inside and look at the plans? You only saw one option. Which I'll admit was the initial plan. It's what I would have done here in the area if I hadn't gotten to know you, and Louise and Nora, Mick, Eddie, and Jimmy, and the girls on the soccer team, and everyone."

"What plans?" she asked, confused. She looked around, but only saw Molly and some stranger. They seemed to be arguing about something. But Molly? Arguing? That was strange.

"Will you let me show you?" Oliver asked, squeezing her hand.

Maggie was confused. "Okay, show me."

He led her into the community center and she was shocked when several of the teenagers high fived him as they passed on their way to the basketball hoops.

She felt his hand on her back and wanted to lean into it. But she couldn't! She had to be strong. She had to put Oliver in her past and... what in the world?

She stared at the big layout set up in the middle of the lobby. It was huge and incredibly detailed. This was similar to the other diorama she'd seen in Oliver's office, but there were differences. There were no skyscrapers. In fact, most of the buildings looked...well, like they looked now. But cleaner. Different. More....interesting! There were trees everywhere. And the abandoned apartment complexes were different. Modernized. She stared. All of the apartments around the neighborhood shared similar traits to what she'd done at Rose Gardens!

"What's this?"

"This is option three," Oliver explained. "You only saw option one that afternoon. Matt was bringing in all three options for my review that day. And this was the winner."

"But...the other buildings," she stammered. "They were bigger. That would mean more business. More profits."

"You've shown me that profits can be made by changing simple things. And taking out the buildings around the neighborhood would change too much. This is a better plan."'

Maggie agreed, but...he would lose so much money. "What about your multi-use ideas?"

He shrugged. "The plans are good. We'll just build that idea in a different area. One that doesn't already have a vibrant community." He sighed and moved closer, taking her hands. "Maggie, my goal isn't to destroy communities. I prefer to go into areas that need help and make things better." He nodded at the plan. "That's what this idea does. It doesn't destroy. It improves and revitalizes, without pushing out the people and families that are the heart of this community."

She blinked, trying to remain tough and in control. But his plans... they sounded lovely! "So, you're not going to tear everything down?"

He pulled her closer. "We're not," he emphasized. "I'm hoping that you will join me in changing things around here. This area has so much potential. The family owned businesses are what so many people crave.

But the store fronts aren't bringing in the business that they could be, if the area was a bit more interesting." He tightened his fingers on hers. "Will you do it, Maggie? Will you help me? Will you work with me to improve things here?"

"Yes," she replied, because there was nothing she'd rather do.

"And will you give me another chance? I know I wasn't completely up front with you about what's going on. But I promise, I wasn't hiding something because I was being nefarious. It was only that I met you and you...well, you blew me away. I'd never met anyone like you. I wanted to get to know you. From the moment you showed up, I was completely lost. And never, *not once,* did I think about using you or spying on anyone. If anything, the residents around here changed my mind, showed me a different way. A better way."

"Yes!" she laughed, tears streaming down her cheeks. Because his words were beautiful!

He moved even closer. "And will you marry me, Maggie? Will you share your life and your dreams with me? Will you grow old with me and make a life with me?"

Maggie's happiness couldn't be contained. "Are you serious?" she whispered.

"Completely serious. I love you, Maggie. I love you and want to spend the rest of my life with you!"

"Yes!" she sobbed. "I love you too. I didn't want to love you. Not after Jerry, but you got to me, Oliver. Damn you!" She couldn't say anything else since he kissed her. And she didn't care that she couldn't finish her thought. Because when he kissed her, every thought flew out of her mind.

Epilogue

Maggie stared at the diorama, not sure what to make of it. "That's interesting," she said, trying to be delicate. "What's this?"

Abigail pulled herself higher, peering into the shoe box. "That's the dinosaur egg," Maggie's seven year old daughter explained.

Gilbreth, their ten year old son, snorted in disgust. "It's just a blob, Abby," he sneered as he passed by, tossing a football in the air and catching it. "Mom, I'm going over to Marcus' house, okay?"

Maggie nodded. "That's fine, but be home in an hour. Dad's cooking dinner tonight."

Gilbreth grunted acknowledgement. "As long as it's not Abby's dinosaur eggs, I'm sure it will be good."

Abby glared at her older brother's retreating back. Maggie knew her daughter wasn't going to let that insult slide.

Thankfully, Oliver appeared, distracting their mischievous daughter. She turned around and smiled, running across the hardwood floors to throw herself into Oliver's arms. "Daddy!" she shrieked joyfully. "Gilly called my dinosaur egg a blob."

Oliver looked around confused as he carried Abigail back into the great room. "And your dinosaur egg is...where?" he asked, glancing at Maggie for clarification.

She pointed to the show box where Abigail had created a scene for her science class. "There," she said, pointing to the blob in the corner.

Oliver admired the box accordingly, silently agreeing that it did look like a blob. "Well, he just doesn't know what dinosaur eggs look like, does he?"

Abby giggled. "You're right! He's just a dumby!"

Oliver's gaze sharpened. "What did I say about calling people names?" he admonished.

Abby sighed. "Sorry Daddy," she said, leaning her head against his shoulder.

Maggie watched the scene play out, rolling her eyes when Abby did the whole "Daddy" routine. She had him wrapped firmly around her little finger. He was such a sucker! But he was her sucker, she thought.

"How are you? Did you have a good day?" Oliver asked Maggie as he set Abby down so she could continue to work on her school assignment.

"I'm doing great!" she replied, wrapping an arm around his waist so she could lean her head against his shoulder. "Dinosaur blobs and all."

He laughed and kissed her. "You're going to explain that to me, right?" he asked, glancing over at the table worriedly.

"Not a chance," Maggie replied, looking as mischievous as her daughter.

Oliver sighed as he tugged at the knot on his tie. "Didn't think so."

And in truth, he wouldn't have it any other way!

A message from Elizabeth:

Thank you ladies! I received a record number of e-mails from all of you after you read "Heated Secrets" and I sincerely hope that Whispered Secrets didn't let you down!

As usual, I'm asking for reviews on your preferred retail site. Reviews are so painfully important and I read all of them. Go back to the retail site's book page – and I thank you – as do so many other readers who are looking for a story to escape from their problems.

(As usual, if you don't want to leave feedback in a public forum, feel free to e-mail me directly at elizabeth@elizabethlennox.com. I answer all e-mails personally, although it sometimes takes me a while. Please don't be offended if I don't respond immediately. I tend to lose myself in writing stories and have a hard time pulling my head out of the book.)

Thank you! Seriously – a big, huge hug for your help in making this book, and all of my stories, a success! I can't do it without you!

Elizabeth

(Keep scrolling for a fun excerpt from next month's "Breathless Secrets"!)

Excerpt from "Breathless Secrets"
Release Date: September 17, 2021

Should he step in and save her?

James Morgan watched the chaotic scene in front of him, listening to the frenzied screams and cringed when another small being galloped around the corner of the building. Ouch! One of them literally jumped on top of the dog pile happening on the ground! That thud looked pretty painful but...what did he know?

Regardless of the person's pain threshold, the maneuver was definitely undignified, he thought, stepping to the side to see the scene from a different angle. Yes, definitely painful. And amusing! Okay, hilarious, he mentally corrected as yet more unruly screams sounded. There were a few noises that seemed to be somewhat maniacal in nature...and some other incongruous sounds that he couldn't identify.

And yet, James continued to stand by the curb, watching the insanity play out with fascination.

A hand reached from the pile of bodies. Should he grab it? Offer assistance? That would be the gentlemanly thing to do.

Probably not a good idea. He didn't want to enter the fray.

He felt someone step up behind him. "Sir, we have a very tight schedule and we don't...," his manager began in a hushed, urgent voice as he moved to stand beside James. But even the never-frazzled Bryan McGregor came to an abrupt halt as he realized what was happening.

Apparently, Bryan's thoughts moved along the same route as James'. "Should we...help maybe?" Bryan asked doubtfully.

James shrugged, angling his head in an effort to make sense of the scene in front of him. "I have no idea," he replied, his tone voicing his confusion.

The screams seemed to grow louder. James peered at the pile of arms and legs from a different angle. Unfortunately, that didn't help and he simply shook his head, sighing with confusion. "It looks a bit painful."

Bryan nodded. "I must agree."

They stood on the sidewalk, watching with horrified fascination.

"*That's* the woman?" James asked, chuckling when a box of...something...was lifted victoriously into the air by a pretty, feminine hand.

Bryan groaned, nodding somberly. "I think so."

James chuckled. "Probably a good thing that the press didn't find out about our excursion today."

Bryan nodded again, watching silently. Both men hissed, visibly cringing, as they watched an elbow slam into an exposed expanse of pale skin. James suspected that the skin was part of the woman's stomach, but he wasn't positive.

"This isn't exactly going as planned," Bryan commented lightly, then pulled his eyes away from the mess of tangled hands and feet, checking his ever present tablet. He touched the screen and James' schedule came up. "We have only ten more minutes here, then you are scheduled to speak at a luncheon for…"

"Bryan," James muttered, stopping his manager's recitation of the day's schedule.

"Yes sir?" Bryan asked, his finger hovering over the tablet.

The corner of James' mouth curled up. "Shut up and let me enjoy this," James muttered.

Bryan blinked, then looked back at the pile of tangled, laughing bodies. With a sigh, Bryan put his tablet behind his back, resigned to James' odd interest.

"I really should help her, shouldn't I?" James asked, his tone almost contemplative.

Bryan shrugged. "I have no idea. You're the one with the manners." James glanced at his friend and manager, one eyebrow lifted in question. Bryan shrugged, grinning as he continued, "I'm the guy with the ruthless personality."

James threw back his head, laughing at Bryan's assessment. He was correct…sort of. "Right," he said, his laughter trailing off slightly. "That's why I won the three billion dollar settlement against that pharma company?"

Bryan grunted, shrugging slightly. "You have your ruthless moments," he acknowledged.

Another man, about the same height as James and Bryan, stepped out of an expensive sedan. The guy looked vaguely familiar, but there was a tension in the man's shoulders that whispered of anger. Or maybe fury? Were the two emotions different?

James turned when the man stepped forward, glancing over at the dog pile of writhing limbs.

"Can I help you?" the guy asked.

James extended his hand. "James Morgan," he greeted the other man. "And you're Oliver Fenton, correct?"

The other man nodded sharply, his eyes narrowing on James. "You're that hot shot attorney, right?"

"That's me," James chuckled, amused as he always was by the various adjectives that people used to describe him. Hot shot? He didn't really consider himself to be that hot. Angry when big companies abused consumers? Yeah. Ready to take on any injustice in the world?

Absolutely! He turned back to the scene on the rough green area that someone might describe as grass, but was really a mix of various weeds that had been mowed to grass height. "I was just..."

The woman in peril suddenly stood up, laughing and pushing her long, blond hair out of her eyes. "Okay!" she declared, laughing. "You guys win!" A moment later, the kids jumped up and down with victorious delight, and greedily held out their hands while the woman distributed...popsicles? The chaotic dog pile was about *popsicles*?

"That's Molly," Oliver explained unnecessarily. "She's the director here at the Center. Would you like an introduction?"

James watched, his lips twitching with amusement as the kids greedily ripped open the paper and joyously started consuming their icy treats. Slowly, they moved away, forming small groups as they perched on the steps of the Center or just crossed their legs and sat down on the green, "grassy" area.

"Yeah," James replied, unable to rip his gaze away from the fascinating woman. She had grass stains on her ragged tee shirt and the soft material hugged her breasts like a loving glove, revealing that the woman had lush curves. The loose jeans rode low on her hips and had definitely seen better days...as well as other owners. They were long and loose around her beautiful hips that weren't slim, but nor would he consider those feminine curves fat either. Her hips were...perfect! Absolutely, amazingly, mouth wateringly perfect!

The man beside James chuckled, and clapped him on the back in a friendly manner. "I know the feeling," he said as he walked away. James couldn't tear his gaze from the laughing beauty. James was content to simply stand here and watch her. Her brown eyes seemed to shimmer with joy and her long hair shimmered around her lovely features which were alive and animated with some sort of inner glow. She seemed so happy, surrounded as she was by the passel of rambunctious children.

His body tightened urgently, wondering what she'd look like with her own children surrounding her. Their children.

That terrifying random thought seemed to shock him out of his lust-induced stupefaction. *His children*? What the hell was he thinking? He didn't have time to date, much less marry and have children! No way! Marriage and children definitely were not on his agenda, he reminded himself. He had a plan for his life. Marriage and children simply weren't in his future.

Bryan sighed and started forward. Despite the uncharacteristic thoughts about marriage and children, James was utterly entranced by the woman. So instead of allowing his manager to start the introductions, James put a hand on Bryan's shoulder. "I've got this," James murmured.

"But…" Bryan hesitated, obviously sensing a deviation. James ignored his manager's startled expression. It wasn't as if he planned to sleep with the woman! He wanted Molly Bradshaw's endorsement for his campaign. A simple enough request, James told himself. Especially considering his competition. The other candidate for the US Senate seat was pathetically lacking in moral character.

Molly closed the cardboard box over the last few popsicles, looking around to ensure that every child had a treat. That's when she spotted the two large men standing on the sidewalk, watching her. Swallowing hard past the sudden tension, her gaze moved from the tall one with the hard jawline to the other man. Then back to the first one.

Both men seemed to have the same sort of demeanor, although the blond man was several inches shorter. They were also roughly equal in brawn, except the muscles looked larger on the taller man. With a mental sigh, Molly acknowledged that it was the first one, the guy with dark brown hair and he blue eyes that caught and held her gaze. He looked as if he should be on the cover of a Hardy Boys book. He was just so…all American. Square jaw, blue eyes, dark hair, broad shoulders, and pristine appearance. He definitely didn't belong in this rough neighborhood. His khaki slacks were freshly ironed and his crisp, white shirt wasn't a dress shirt, but was made of that thick, no-iron cotton that could only be found at high-end stores. The kind of store that Molly couldn't afford to walk into, much less buy from.

And yet, for all of his good-boy looks and clothing, there was something…bad-boyish about him. While the man next to him looked as if he might be funny in a ruthless sort of way, the tall, devastatingly handsome "good-boy"…definitely *wasn't* a good boy. Nope. He was naughty. The look in his eyes whispered that he had some very wicked tendencies.

Fortunately, Molly didn't have time for those games. With extreme control, she ripped her gaze away from the man and looked around at her kids. They weren't exactly "her" children. But she considered them to be under her protection. They lived in this neighborhood and were here at the Community Center for the last few days of summer vacation before school started back up. She loved these kids. Ensuring that they were safe and well educated, even fed when needed, was her mission in life. Her calling. Her vocation, some might say.

"Molly Bradshaw?" a deep voice called out.

Molly cringed. She wanted to ignore that sexy voice, but her kids looked up curiously when the tall stranger said her name. Unfortunately, Molly wasn't just their protector, she was also their mentor. Molly knew that she had to model good behavior, even during those moments when she seriously wanted to run and hide.

So, Molly turned and pasted a bright, friendly smile on her face.

Blinking and tilting her head way back, she braced herself for...whatever might come next. And she was pretty sure that she wasn't going to like whatever it was!

"Yes? How can I help you?" she asked as politely as possible.

"I'm James Morgan," he said, extending his hand.

That name rang a bell in her mind. She extended her hand, trying to remember where she'd heard that name before. But for the life of her, she couldn't place him. She'd definitely never met him before. She would have remembered a guy that handsome and tall and...terrifying.

Remembering her manners, and the curious eyes watching their interaction, she shook the man's hand. "It's lovely to meet you, Mr. Morgan," she replied formally.

"It's great to meet you as well," he replied. "I've heard a lot about you."

Molly blinked, surprised. "You have?" Her eyebrows shot up. "How?"

He laughed and she couldn't stop the shiver of awareness that rolled over her. His laugh was deep and incredibly sexy.

"You're the director of this community center."

"That's right," she confirmed, nodding slightly.

"You've done some amazing things in the neighborhood."

Molly wasn't comfortable claiming credit for the outstanding programs happening at the Center. "Oh, the changes around here aren't mine," Molly asserted firmly. "The entire community came together to right the wrongs of the past," she corrected.

His grin widened. "You're being modest, Ms. Bradshaw." He looked around, winking at a group of kids who were still enjoying their popsicles. "From what I've read, you've initiated a great many programs for the community that have–"

"We should take this inside," Molly interrupted stiffly. "How about if we go into my office?"

He looked confused, but nodded. "That would be fine," he said. "Lead the way."

Molly gritted her teeth, frustration almost overwhelming her. Was it just frustration or crushing disappointment? No! That's ridiculous! She couldn't be disappointed that the gorgeous man was here to sell her something. Ugh!

But Molly knew the type. He wanted something, either from her or from the Center. She didn't know which yet, but he clearly wasn't here for kicks and giggles. Looking around, she spotted Mary, one of the youth volunteers. "Mary, can you get the kids ready for afternoon practice?"

Mary quickly agreed, then trotted over to the younger kids, three other teenagers trailing behind her. "Sure, Molly. I think its belly-ball today, right?"

Molly shot a glance at the man, praying he had no idea what "belly ball" was. "I think so. I'll make sure to send someone out with the equipment." Turning back to Mr. All American, she nodded towards the Center's entrance. "This way, Mr. Morgan."